HER GRUMPY BOSS

CARMEN TATE

Published by Blushing Books
An Imprint of
ABCD Graphics and Design, Inc.
A Virginia Corporation
977 Seminole Trail #233
Charlottesville, VA 22901

Carmen Tate
Her Grumpy Boss

eBook ISBN: 978-1-63954-031-0
Print ISBN: 978-1-63954-032-7
v1

Chapter 1

A chorus of sputtering and spitting worked together with the frustration of the Buick's owner who was in the process of swearing at the ignition. Under normal circumstances, she logically understood talking to a vehicle did nothing to encourage proper functioning. However, these were not normal circumstances and she didn't have time to be dealing with this. She shoved the driver's side door open.

Opening her apartment front door, with fingers crossed that her roommate didn't have any plans, she shouted, "Hey, Katie! Could you do me a huge favor?"

The girl popped her head around the corner. "Depends on what you're asking, crazy."

"My car won't start, and I'm supposed to be meeting some guy for drinks in fifteen minutes."

"Sure, I'll take you... will I need to pick you up too?"

"Depends on if he makes a good impression or not. C'mon though! Being late more than five to ten minutes goes from fashionable to tacky really quickly."

Katie grabbed her keys from the hook and the two of them practically raced to her car. As she passed from sidewalk to parking lot, her heel got stuck in a crack and she went tumbling.

Her roommate laughed... a lot, but she was too irritated to see how funny the situation was. Righting herself, she declared, "We need to leave a note at the office. We are way too pretty to have to deal with this broken up parking lot."

At the bar, she was nearly stampeded by an anxious guy with a phone in his hand. She had barely entered the building. I mean, she was hot, but damn. Could he be a little more chill about it?

"Are you Jennifer Caman from Cupid Match?"

"Er, no. I'm not, sorry." It bothered her to lie, but she knew it would bother her much more to sit and have a conversation with this man for an entire drink. He was wearing dirty, work boots on a first date!

"Are you sure? You look a little bit like the girl in the photo. You're not meeting anyone?"

"No, sorry. I'm just here to sit by myself and have a drink. I've had a pretty rough day. How late is your date? If she's more than fifteen minutes late, I'd just assume she's not coming and save yourself the hassle."

Thank God, her Cupid Match photo was from when she was still blonde.

Jennifer sat at the bar and ordered herself a cosmopolitan. Granted, now she was going to be paying for this drink herself and wouldn't be able to get a coffee before school again for the next three weeks. However, she couldn't just leave now.

"Couldn't help overhearing... why are you having a bad day?" The bartender asked after delivering her cocktail.

"My car isn't starting, and I need to find a job, but I'll be all right. I always am."

"Can you bartend? We're hiring here!"

"Thanks for the offer, but that's not the sort of job I mean." People didn't understand. She lived – er, wanted to live – too luxuriously to just accept any old job. Bartending would not look good on her resume.

She just needed to get in with a wealthier crowd...

Her train of thought was cut short as the bell above the entrance dinged. Her young heart raced and her stomach turned into butterfly knots as she glanced over her shoulder to see the mysterious man entering through the bar's front door. He was the most gorgeous man she had ever seen in her twenty-one years of life. She shocked herself by maintaining a brief, but memorable moment of eye contact with the stranger. Typically, men who were clearly out of her league made her cower and hide. This unlikely interaction was the one exception. Before she knew it, she had offered a timid smile. Even more surprising was the kind reaction she received from him. His eyes crinkled in a return smile.

Man, was he something to look at: tanned skin, muscular arms held tight by a short sleeve shirt, and those eyes... She couldn't wait to tell her friends about him.

Now, that it was the next day, she couldn't decide whether or not to tell her girlfriends about the man from the bar. She had this horrible habit of getting her hopes up too soon and didn't want to deal with any lectures from her well-meaning pals. They wouldn't see it as anything special, she was a little bit boy crazy after all, but that right there had to be proof this had been different. He was clearly a man, not some boy.

She had lost herself in thought and when she came back down to earth, Jenn found herself to be still maneuvering her hairdressing mannequin's coarse hair into thick rollers. How she had managed to keep on working without dropping anything was a mystery, but she had to admit she was quite proud of herself for being so slick.

Where had her girls gone off to? This was always happening on her more daydream-y and unfocused days. She would get lost in the work she had at hand, look around, and realize her clique had been long gone, probably off to wax someone's coochy or shampoo each other's hair for the fourth time this week.

Jennifer had decided to tell them when she saw them coming back from the secluded shampoo room. Lola had a bleach stained towel tied into a knot at the back of her head and was settling into a chair while Mikayla plugged her blow-dryer into the adjacent station's outlet.

Steph was trailing behind and looking like she needed something to do with her hands. She was most likely 'helping' Mikayla with the project of styling Lola's hair. She had to give Steph a bit of credit, however. It was quite possible Mikayla might need assistance as Lola's hair was a pain in the ass to work with. Her hair was much longer than the others' and there was also the added challenge of working around her tape-in extensions. Lola would usually end up brushing them herself as they were easily tangled and all of us were afraid of ripping one out.

"What's that excited look for?" Lola asked me with a hint of laughter already streaking across her pretty face. She was definitely the friend who Jennifer would save the most ridiculous of stories for.

"You're not going to believe me, but I fell in love and I think we're going to need to start planning a wedding as soon as humanly possible."

"You're crazy, with who?" her loyal friend replied, not a trace of shock invading her tone. Big proclamations like this were obviously typical for mid-Tuesday conversation headlines.

"You know how I was meeting that guy for drinks on Friday? Total loser, showed up with work boots on, but another guy came in and bought me a drink. He was absolutely perfect and he was wearing a suit! He didn't stay very long, but we're meeting there again this Friday."

"Sounds exciting. What's his name?"

You know, you'd think she would've asked that...

As much as Jenn wanted to sit around and think about her upcoming date, she knew she couldn't set everything else aside, like her job hunt. She had to find the right salon for her, one where she'd make good money and be surrounded by the right people.

Jenn had scheduled herself to attend a class at Gilberts Salon today. She had visited a slew of salons in the past few weeks, and each one had presented its own red flags within the first fifteen minutes of her visit. Everything from something as minor as not offering the textured-hair services to being straight up nasty and leaving her with a horrible feeling in the pit of her stomach. Those trips had left her wondering if she had gotten herself into the wrong line of work.

During the entire drive she reflected on how lucky she should feel having been invited to attend this class, as it was mainly for Gilberts' staff, and there was the potential she would be one of the only attendees who didn't have her cosmetology license. She took it as a compliment they had thought of her in the first place.

She followed her GPS, instructing her to turn right into a parking lot that was part of a strip mall. This struck her as strange as she had previously imagined Gilberts as an upscale salon. But here it was appearing the same, from the outside, as any old nail salon.

As she parked, a Range Rover pulled in next to her on the left. Her 1999 rusty Buick wasn't able to put up a fight in contrast to this sexy vehicle. She reminded herself she should just be happy she was getting herself out of her comfort zone and doing things like this, while her fellow classmates made a desperate effort to make it to school on time, and to do so without their shower caps still covering their cheap weaves.

She and the other driver both made their way towards the salon. Instead of thinking of her inferiority, she chose to see this woman as an example of what her prospective future looked like.

Jenn was content with a seat in the back. The expansive room was already filled with chattering stylists. You'd be crazy not to admit that simply being in a room with this many beauty queens was overwhelming. Hairstylists are known for their big personalities and the room was just about bursting with the energy that was bubbling up and over. Jenn noticed her new friend had decided to sit by her, still keeping her distance with a seat in between them. They were clearly not adjacent seats level yet.

"Hey, I'm Ashley. I hope you don't mind me sitting by you. Have you ever been to Gilberts before?" The brunette made her introduction.

"Oh, gosh. Is it that obvious I'm a newbie?"

"Well, I was in your same place three years ago when I came to one of these things by myself, too. So I think I kind of sniffed you out because I remember that feeling so vividly. Also, your hair case does say 'Levitation Beauty Academy' so I kind of assumed you were still a student." She laughed. "I remember being nervous too so you're okay. You can relax."

The room quieted as a man walked to the front. "Welcome to Gilberts. I do understand we have some students who have come to learn with us and I would like to take a second to recognize each of them."

He called off four names and had the ladies stand up as the room greeted them. None of the names had been 'Jennifer' and Ashley took it upon herself to fix that.

"Oh, we have another in the back. This is Jennifer."

The room kind of heard, but kind of didn't. It was an awkward ordeal and Jenn wished they would've just let it slide. At that moment, Mrs. Gilbert apologized to her.

"I'm sorry. I had no idea you were coming."

"It's all right. You and your husband teach a business class at Levitation once a month. We were introduced there, remember?"

It was an uncomfortable conversation to be having in front of the entire room. Mrs. Gilbert nodded as if she remembered, while it was obvious to everyone that she had, in fact, not remembered.

Halfway through the day, Jenn had resigned herself to the fact she would have to reach out to other salons. This was after listening to many covert and outright jabs to her self-esteem. Playing their due part were comments about how she needed to figure out what she wanted because there was no way you could do hair and work in fashion as well. There was also an insult dressed up as constructive criticism in which the guilty party nearly convinced her she should never wear glasses again as they only served to emphasize the fact her profile was not symmetrical and, therefore, not ideal. The rest of the day she spent pretending to listen and be attentive while she was really fantasizing about fucking the man from the bar. You could say she didn't learn much.

How had that girl from the bar managed to catch his attention with just her smile? Was he that desperate to get laid he would spend his time thinking about some otherwise unworthy-of-note girl? Hell, she could've been half his age, but business had been such a headache as of late. He had taken to coming home completely and utterly alone so as to not have to deal with anymore meaningless drama. You would think working with some of San Francisco's hottest stylists would be any man's wet dream, but not in Anthony's case. However, it would be a lie if he didn't acknowledge the fact having her petite and appealing frame instead of his usual glass of bourbon this evening was all too tempting. He tried not to despise himself for it, but those big eyes full of innocence had been refreshing.

He couldn't permit himself to be distracted, but here he was continuing to fantasize about a young woman as his unaware business partner sat rambling on about finances and budgets. His partner deserved much greater respect than that, but he just couldn't help himself.

He could not wait to meet her again.

Chapter 2

"**Y**ou're not allowed to leave my bed until I've given you permission to do so."

Jennifer Caman felt her breath catch in her throat, startled by both what he said as well as by the fact the handsome devil was awake. She was halfway out the bedroom door with a blanket held up to cover herself. She thought for sure the man beside her would be too hungover to sense her absence as she made her way to the bathroom and to get the hell out of there. Don't get her wrong, she liked the guy and had a fantastic night. However, she was very wary of him. The way he spoke to her both aroused her and frightened her at the same time. He wasn't the sort she would usually get romantic with. In her mind, she was just making a graceful exit from a one-night stand.

She didn't know how to respond. On the one hand, she wanted to crawl back into bed with him and go for another round, but her mind told her to run. Play it cool.

"I'm sorry to wake you. I was just looking for your bathroom."

He didn't give much away, but his eyes spoke for him as if

to say, "Tell me the truth or there will be consequences." He lay there with one muscular arm behind his neck and plush bed sheets covering the lower half of him. He took his time before forming a response. Jenn wasn't sure if she should continue leaving or if she was waiting for him to speak. He made her sweat. She hated how in control of the situation he was. Why had she come home with him when she could've just taken him back to her apartment? She should've just said no to the hook-up altogether. She knew nothing about him. She honestly couldn't even remember what he had said his name was. Adam? Jonathan? If she hadn't known her roommate had her exact location, she might've dialed 911. How did all the women in the movies do this like it was no big deal?

When she felt she couldn't wait another second, he made his calculated response.

"Down the hall to the left."

As she turned to head in that direction, she realized her blanket shield was doing nothing to protect her backside that was now on display for him, cheeks tensing with each tippy-toe step.

She had to give it to him. The man had an extremely sexy loft-style apartment. His walls were dark, some were painted black and there was dim lighting throughout the home. It made it seem like the Adonis ate, slept, and breathed sex. Her bare feet padded across the cool, wood floor. It wasn't far to the first door on the left. Wrapping her palm around the knob and turning, she gasped and jumped back. Instead of a bathroom she had stepped into a walk-in closet about the size of a half bath. The light was already on. Had he planned it that way? There were a plethora of leather gadgets and gizmos, clamps and whips, handcuffs and vibrators. She felt heat rising through her while her stomach dropped. The back wall was basically a shrine to spanking. She recognized many of the devices that could be used for

BDSM purposes, whether she had seen them before online or in a store or in her imagination didn't matter. If he thought he would be using any of that stuff on her, he would be sorely mistaken. Even as she made the resolution, she felt heat pooling between her legs. Her pussy clearly didn't agree with her and she could feel wetness on her naked inner thigh.

She wasn't sure what the appropriate reaction to this scenario was, let alone if she could bring herself to react at all. Could she get by pretending she hadn't seen what she had? If she wasn't spooked before, she definitely was now.

"You said on the left?"

She heard him chuckling from his bedroom. Had he done that on purpose? He should've told her he was a freak while they had still been at the bar as opposed to springing it on her like this when she was already attempting a getaway. She could only blame herself. Last night, she noticed the hooks at the head and foot of his bed but had been too drunk to care.

"Did I say left? My bad. The bathroom is on the right."

Pee and leave. Pee and leave. Pee and leave, she kept repeating to herself. She hurriedly shut the door behind her and locked it. She could hear him climbing out of bed as she used the toilet. She would just make the excuse she had a stomachache and needed to get going. Drying her hands on the towel at the back of the door, she held her shoulders back and her head high. She could reject this gorgeous, kinky man and get on with the rest of her life. She knew she could.

He made her jump, again. He was standing right outside the bathroom door, waiting for her. He was wearing briefs and his socks. What the hell was he doing and why was he so fucking cute? As creeped out as she was, there was still a desire within her for him to push her to her knees right then and there. Maybe, this could be fun?

"I can't say that was the best response I've ever gotten.

Most women love to see my toys. What makes you so different?"

She couldn't help feeling a little embarrassed. She believed him. Most women were much more open and experimental than she was. She just never thought she would be able to get over herself and how dirty she would feel for wanting those things. Maybe, it's how she was raised. Even if she were to play with the darker side of sex, she always felt it should be with someone you're very comfortable with. She couldn't say that she was with her John Doe.

"I'm not like that. Will you please just let me get my clothes?"

She watched as the charming green eyes went from playful and curious to irritated. He was like a schoolboy who was just told no to a second round of dessert.

"I'd prefer if you stayed how you are."

Her stomach flopped. Why couldn't she find it in herself to say no to him? Was she weak? In one fluid and domineering motion, she found herself scooped into his bronzed arms. When he picked her up, the blanket fell. She was completely naked before him in the morning light. He didn't seem to mind and carried her back to his room.

"Let's have a little chat and then you can choose to leave if you wish." She melted. Muscular arms did have a tendency to make her soft in the knees. He climbed onto the tall bed with her still in his arms. Leaning against the headboard, he sat with her in his lap. What was the worst that could happen, he spanks her before sending her on her way? She thought she'd survive.

"So you're not like that, huh? From what you were whispering to me at the club last night, I thought for sure you were. If you're not experienced, you must be curious. I'm a very good Dom and could go easy on you as I show you the ropes. What do you think? Talk to me."

Jenn sat and thought about his proposition, wondering if he had used the phrase 'show you the ropes' as a pun. Her index fingernail resting on her bottom front teeth as it did when she got nervous.

"Slow down, big guy. I don't think I'm into all of that. I'm a nice, clean girl. Besides, why would I experiment with you? I barely know you. I bet you don't even remember what my name is." Staring into his green eyes, her heart pounded so hard she could feel it throbbing in her temples. Not only did he get her pulse racing, but she also felt like she was on fire, which was weird because she had goosebumps and the wetness between her legs was now bringing a coolness. Her body contradicted itself. Her heart contradicted itself, but her head held a firm no. What would her friends think of her if they found out how dark her fantasies could go? She would be ashamed.

"Jennifer Caman, you are one confusing young woman. I think you need to admit what you want and stop judging yourself for wanting it, because I hear what you're saying with your mouth and yet, here you are, wrapped in my arms after having seen my naughty sex closet. There is also another factor I have to consider. You do know you're sitting on my lap naked, right? I can feel how wet you are for me." With this last remark, he thrust his forefinger deep inside her before immediately withdrawing. He was obviously trying to further prove his point and he was succeeding.

"Are you scared of me?"

Be honest, Jenn. Go in. "How could I not be? I'm in bed with a man who is much older than me, who I've only known for one night, who wants me to surrender myself to him or whatever, and who wants to do all kinds of crazy shit to me— whipping, beating, heaven knows what."

"Wait, did you just say 'heaven knows what'? Who cares if there's a big age gap between us? You're an old lady at heart.

Here's how this works: We go slow and simple, starting with things like blindfolds and handcuffs. Every time we try something new, we will discuss it beforehand. You should know I will push you to go further than you think you can, but you will have a safe word you can use at any time. It doesn't matter how big or small you feel your reason is, you say your safe word and all play immediately stops. I will want to talk about whatever upset you and after every experience, we will talk about what you liked and what you didn't like. This helps me make sure our play continues to be pleasurable and exciting for both you and me."

Did she dare test the waters? What if she hates everything he tries and he becomes resentful towards her? She had to admit though... she loved trying new things and, even though she was only twenty-one, vanilla sex was becoming just that: vanilla.

It had been twelve days since Jennifer spent the night with her mysterious master of kink and try as she might not to, here she was wondering about him... again. She was in a business class being given by the Gilberts. She allowed her sinful mind to run rampant.

As the multitude of students began to either vacate in haste or schmooze with the Gilberts, Jennifer noticed Mr. Ben had entered with searching eyes. It appeared she had been the student he was looking for.

"Hey, Jennifer. Could I have a brief word with you in the hall?" Mr. Ben asked, causing a panic to take form within her.

Jennifer felt she had a good relationship with Mr. Ben, even considered him a friend, but she couldn't help being anxious to hear what he might have to say. Even though Jennifer was one of the kindest students in the school and had been awarded the title of 'Miss Congeniality' in a vote by her classmates, she was still leery. In a school full of many different women, it was normal you would offend somebody – both by accident and on purpose, depending on what kind of person you fancy yourself to be at the time – especially if you had as big a personality as Jenn had. It also wouldn't be unrealistic to suspect someone could've tattled to Mr. Ben in secret for just about anything. Bitches could be petty.

"What's up? I'm not in trouble, am I?" Jenn laughed a halfhearted laugh, showing she was only half kidding.

"Oh no, silly, of course not." Mr. Ben flipped his hand as if brushing this idea away. Mr. Ben had such a quirky personality. It was easy for her to smile around him and she enjoyed the few chances she would get when they could talk about how much they loved Lady Gaga or about the hairstyling for their favorite shows. He even told her personal things about his husband and son, which didn't help Jennifer's ego. Then he started explaining.

"Quite the opposite, actually. When you enrolled here at Levitation, you also signed an agreement to be scouted by Mrs. Giuliani who, as you know, owns this school. She keeps an eye on students' work by checking out the school's social media and by conferring with your educators to see where they believe your capability falls. This is all done in the hopes of finding a student for her Prodigy Program, which you were selected for this year." He had a look of both pride and something that could only be described as kudos on his face. She would consider him to be one of her mentors so she supposed he could be allowed to feel a sense of pride over her accomplishments.

So her hard work had been seen! She had been feeling like there was no point to her hustle as it had gone seemingly unnoticed. There was just one question.

"That's amazing! But— er... Mr. Ben? What is the prodigy program?"

"Not to worry. I have a packet here with all the information you need, but basically it's an elite assistant job. The first thing you need to do is call and set up a day for your interview. If the interview goes well, things are likely to become more official and you can sign your contract. The phone number for the front desk at their business office is on the first page. Their lovely receptionist will forward you to whichever Giuliani is available at the time." Mr. Ben handed her the packet with a wink and took off down the hall.

Chapter 3

J enn sat at the edge of her bed, nervously staring at the packet on her lap. She knew she needed to hurry up and make the call. It wasn't even that big of a deal. Who knows? Maybe they made a mistake and had meant to choose another student, but it was starting to get to that point in her education where she needed a salon to send her clients to so they could follow her after graduation. She had planned on calling Giuliani's, but now her nerves were much more intense.

Before she knew what was happening, the packet was at the cluttered bottom of her nightstand's junk drawer. She didn't understand where all the nerves were coming from. She had already spoken with so many different salon owners the experience had become relatively easy. Jenn wasn't the sort of girl to shy away from interviews. They were the one scenario where many of her best qualities came to light. The only possible explanation for her uncalled-for hesitance was her own self-doubt and her chronic discontent. She had a bad habit of avoiding opportunities that might actually be good for her. It was blatant self-sabotage, really. If she never took the chance, she could never ruin it.

This did seem to be exactly what she was looking for… so, with that thought, Jenn made the resolution to call Giuliani's. She readied herself for the call. She had already decided how she was going to play it: cool, calm, and collected.

There it was as if she did not know it was about to happen or that she was the one initiating it: the nerve-wracking dial tone. With a quick click of the receiver, there was a chirpy voice piercing her ear with an over enthusiastic greeting.

"Office of the Giulianis, Candace speaking, how can I make your day just a teensy-weensy bit better?"

"Hi, my name is Jennifer Caman. I'm currently a student at Levitation Beauty Academy and I wanted to talk to the Giulianis about their Prodigy Program."

"Please, hold." Well, that was abrupt. She must not have a cheesy line memorized for this particular scenario.

"Hello." The voice was deep and smooth like dark chocolate that's still warm and hadn't yet been formed into perfect shaped little squares. Jenn's breath hitched in her throat as if a sudden gate decided to cover up her windpipe and it was hard to form introductory words, even though the contents of the conversation to come were quite simple, really.

"Hey." The tiny word barely came out and the weird sound it made could only be described as a raspy whisper yell. She mentally kicked herself for using such a lazy and informal word. Why didn't she say something like 'Hello' or 'Hi'? Embarrassed, but somehow managing to pull herself out of it, she continued. "I'm Jennifer Caman, from Levitation Beauty Academy. I'm calling because I was selected for your Prodigy Program and would like to set up an interview."

His returning response came back unexpected and cryptic as a drastic parallel to how kind and sweet he had sounded just seconds before. "Who gave you this number? I am not the one to speak to about this. You will need to call one of the salon locations as opposed to our business office."

"I-I'm sorry. The director of my school spoke to me and gave me this number."

"Listen, little girl. I don't pay much attention to students, much less schedule interviews. You most likely need to speak to my mother. Good day to you."

Little girl? Sure, he's a successful, wealthy, powerful, possible gazillionaire... but really? Who the hell does he think he is?

"But—" Jenn's sentence was deemed irrelevant as she realized he had hung up on her. She was shocked. She had just wanted to be polite and ask for the proper number to call so as not to waste any more of his time. Hopefully, Google would be a bit friendlier to her than he had been, but why had he seemed so familiar?

Jenn tugged at the hem of her pink pencil skirt. It was going to be one of those days where she would need to find a way to be discrete as she slid her skirt back down every few minutes. Sure, a hairstylist has to follow certain standards and wear all black everything when on the job, but that didn't mean it was necessary for her to pretend to be boring for the interview. She slipped her pointed-toe, glossy, black pumps over her pedicured toes, grasping the stiff back of the shoe and pulling it up over her heel. In a moment of unashamed confidence, she stood looking at herself in the full-body mirror that hung on her closet door and she felt damn good. Her skirt clung to her ass in just the right way. Her button up was tucked into the silky skirt, giving a cinched effect at her waist. It all served to better enhance her curvy, grown woman figure. On top of all that, the coordination of her black shirt and shoes served to show she still respected the all black uniform to an extent.

Outfit aside, she had always been fantastic in interviews and she knew this meeting would not be the outlier. Even though the other salons she had taken a look at hadn't been the right fit for her, that didn't mean she didn't suit them. Most of the places had offered her an assistant position on the spot, even the ones who had made snide remarks about her glasses and ambitions. There were also a couple who had suggested she skip the whole assisting process and start out with her own chair, but the reality of these bold offers was most salons in this area were desperate for new talent.

On arriving at Giuliani's, things were already looking more promising than they had at any of the previous places she'd visited. In comparison with the ghetto location of Gilberts, Giuliani's had a fresh air to it as it was situated in the bustling center of downtown and had its own private parking in the back of the building. Stepping through that front door felt like crossing through to another planet. It was like you could feel the creative and inspiring energy just zinging off the walls. Based off her first impression, the stylists were boldly diverse in appearance and you know what else? Not one of them were wearing head-to-toe black. Many different cultural backgrounds were represented.

Jenn stepped up and introduced herself to the older woman at the black marbled desk, understanding if she were to make Giuliani's her future salon, she would need to have the front desk team as a useful ally. Offering a big smile she hoped didn't seem too fake, she made her first move. "Hi, I'm Jennifer Caman. I have an interview at 2 o'clock with Monica." As the words, left her mouth she reached out for a quick handshake, Alex-and-Ani bracelets jingling as she did so. This quaint sound served as an additive to the aura she was attempting to create about herself.

"You're ten minutes early. Color me impressed. Not so early that it's irritating, but still showing how prompt you can be." A smile of approval was exchanged as she offered her hand to shake. "I'm Monica. You can follow me this way and we can get started. Would you like a water?"

"That would be great, thank you." Her mouth had gone a tad dry, come to think of it.

"Flat or bubbly?" Was this woman joking? Jenn had died and gone to hair heaven where she had a vision of herself twenty years from now performing a haircut and laughing with her client, *still* working at Giuliani's.

"Is that even a question? Bubbly, of course," she answered the question with a laugh and any little bit of nerves she had felt at the start of the day disintegrated. She felt at home as she took her seat at the station nearby and waited for the woman to return.

Monica didn't take long to return with a bottle of unflavored Perrier. "I wanted to do your interview in our loft space. It looks out over all of the stylist stations so while we chat you can have a look and get a feel for what our staff, clients, and atmosphere are like." She led Jenn up a spiraling staircase to an area that appeared to be reserved for nail services. Monica sat at a station and Jenn took the seat on the other side, facing her.

They talked about everything. It was nothing like your normal interview. Of course, the usual topics and questions were discussed and asked, but it didn't take long for the two to dive into deeper conversation. If someone were to peer in and observe, it would seem much more like two long lost friends meeting for coffee than an interview. Monica didn't hesitate to share the story of how she had decided to join Giuliani's, which then turned into the story of her entire career journey thus far. Jenn sat in rapt attention, soaking up every word and allowing it to get her excited about the future and all the opportunities and stories she was sure to have waiting for her after graduation.

During the conversation, Jenn did take a few glances to see what was happening on the salon floor. She made eye contact with a few of the stylists and every interaction built an intuitive gut feeling, driving her to become a part of Giuliani's that very day. You could tell the other stylists wanted the opportunity to meet her and the idea of fresh meat didn't set off any warning sirens of competition, but a gift of someone new to bounce ideas off of. Everyone seemed busy and they, by no means, were needy for new clients. Noticing the amount of people coming in and out of the door confirmed to her she would be able to build a booming career here.

In the middle of explaining how she wanted to eventually work in the fashion industry as a creative director over a clothing brand while still working behind the chair, Monica's facial expression had an abrupt switch. Her look went from full attention on Jennifer to a hint of confusion and then, automatic seriousness as Jenn ventured to guess that someone was now standing over her shoulder.

Caught mid-thought, Jenn turned to take a glimpse over her shoulder and there he was— in all of his sensual Italian glory. She soaked up every inch of him. His sheer height made her shiver and those green eyes really were piercing. Her arms sprinkled with goosebumps while her ears inflamed at the same time. How could just looking at this man make her body react this way? She was able to watch him walk towards them in slow motion. Her intake didn't stop at his eyes. She used this slow-motion moment to her fullest advantage. His business casual attire was perfectly tailored to his beefy body. His sleeves were rolled up, only far enough to see the veins that were displayed there, evidence of his brute strength. Jenn was thankful for the men's fashion of today because the navy chinos he was wearing draped over him better than any pair of pants Jenn owned herself, but what the fuck was he doing here?

"Oh, Mr. Giuliani, I had no idea you would be in today. I won't have those sheets you asked for organized until tomorrow afternoon." Monica was panicking by the sound of her voice and Jenn felt disappointment over her new friend. He's just a super-hot, powerful, superior of yours. What's the big deal? Backtrack a couple seconds, did she say 'Mr. Giuliani'? He must've lied to Jenn at the bar then because there was no way someone could be both 'Francesco Fregoli' and 'Mr. Giuliani'. How had he come up with such a convincing alias?

"We'll still have our meeting as scheduled, Ms. Bailey. For now, I would like to have a word with Ms. Caman. Her interview may reconvene after I've spoken with her in private." Why does he want to speak with her and why did it have to be in private?

"Yes, sir." Monica stumbled over herself getting out of her seat, desperate to make herself scarce.

"You can stay here, Monica. Ms. Caman and I will be in the office." Jenn stood, almost stumbling due to the tightness of her skirt. She tugged it downwards, too nervous to try and make it less obvious what she was doing. Anthony took her by the wrist, dragging her with him towards the spiral staircase. The force of the gesture came as a shock and her heels almost became her demise.

He led her down the staircase with Jenn's heart thumping so hard it could've come up her esophagus and hopped onto the metal edges of the steps. What is happening right now? Is this a dream or, perhaps, a nightmare? Francesco – er – Mr. Giuliani was hard to read, and it made her feel like she was in trouble, about to receive a detention or another crueler punishment of some sort. What she had done wasn't the only mystery seeing as she clearly knew nothing about the man she was seeing.

His strong, un-calloused hand was still constricting her wrist. Weren't men who were as muscular as him supposed to have rough hands from lifting barbells or whatever? He had been pulling Jenn down a narrow hallway and there was no putting a finger on what she was feeling. She couldn't be scared because what could he possibly do to her in a salon filled with both employees and clients? The answer was a lot.

He slammed the large oak door behind them, and she found herself in a small office, simply an executive desk and three chairs. Mr. Giuliani locked the door behind him, only further raising Jenn's suspicions that something bad was about to happen. Why was there even a lock on the door? Within seconds, he was pressed against her, his hot breath moistening the back of her neck. His hand was no longer around her wrist but both were now grasping her hips. His hold on her was firm as if to say, "You're staying here whether you like it or not". Jenn was overwhelmed. Honestly, how had she not passed out?

"I usually abstain from relations with employees. Think you can keep your mouth shut?" She couldn't hold her shudder in. Her pulse was racing and to her surprise, her clit was throbbing. Most men couldn't turn her on like this even with their dick inside her.

She nodded her head, but that wasn't good enough. "I want to hear you say it. Now." The urgency in his voice had her adrenaline rushing.

"I can keep my mouth shut." The voice didn't sound like her own. Her sharp tongue that didn't back down had deserted her and what was left was something that resembled a timid girl mouthing the words 'Trick or Treat' on a stranger's doorstep.

"Good girl. Have you thought about what you'd like your safe word to be?"

"Apricots? I stole it from a movie."

"Apricots it is."

His hand made its way to the baby hairs at the nape of her neck within seconds and he manipulated her open mouth towards his. This man pulled hair like he did everything else; he meant business. The kiss reminded her of the hello she had received across the phone. It was hot and passionate and, even though she knew she shouldn't, she went back in for more. With him still behind her, her ass rubbed against his dick and she finally felt like she could read him. She was doing the same thing to him that he was doing to her.

His right hand that rested over her hip looped around lower and sneakily found her inner thigh. He scrunched the pencil skirt up as he trailed higher. His touch was light. Thank goodness she shaved above the knee today. Once he reached his destination, there was no more gentleness or hesitancy. His three middle fingers found the source of her arousal and made rough, jarring circles through her panties. She bit her lip, not on purpose, but in an effort to keep herself quiet as well as to hide her shock at his brazenness.

His firm grasp returned to both her wrists, one in each hand. He folded her arms behind her and moved to hold them there with just one hand as he slid the papers from the large, wooden desk to the floor. Arms still held in place, he bent her over the desk. Her skirt was still a little out of place and he finished the job by sliding the pink material completely over her hips, exposing her creamy skin and thong beneath.

"Don't move," he commanded. She didn't voice any of her questions, but rather did as she was told, lying with her chest firmly pressed to oak and her round ass on display. She made sure to not move her hands from behind her back, not knowing what sort of punishment she might receive if she didn't stay completely in the place he had left her.

She could hear the sound of him undoing his belt buckle and quickly after, the sound of metal clinking onto the floor. Jenn turned her head to catch sight of the Dom, only to be reprimanded and told to 'face the wall'. This wasn't before getting a glimpse of his erection and of him with a packaged condom in hand. It was cold waiting for him, except for her face and her inflamed cheeks. She picked up the sound of latex being rolled over her lover's shaft.

Grabbing onto her placed wrists and tugging her upwards and off the desk, he whispered into her ear, "You ready?" She had no time to answer. He slid her thong to the side and rammed into her wet pussy. His dick was perfect, no awkward attempts to get it in, only one powerful thrust. She couldn't believe how amazing it felt to have him inside her again. She was so wet for him and with such little foreplay. Her hips were firmly pressed to the desk, but the rest of her hovered. He was holding her up by a fisted hand, tangled deep into her hair and another at her waist. He pulled her hair tighter with each thrust and her eyes were in line with the ceiling. He pulled her further back to kiss her on the forehead before moving his hand to her throat. He made this transition quick, not allowing her tits to feel the desk's surface once more. It was a gentle hold, but it had forced a moan from her lips.

The hand he had at her waist moved to cover her mouth while the other tightened around her throat. The message was clear. 'Keep your mouth shut'. He continued to ram into her, his pace never easing up. His hips moved in a perfect cadence and if her moan hadn't been heard by any employees, she was convinced the sound of her ass repeatedly smacking into his thighs would be.

She felt like her arousal was just about to reach its peak

when he withdrew himself from her, gave her clit a light smack, stepped back into his pants, and did up his buckle.

Just like that, it was over. She stood there by herself beside the desk, pink skirt still over her hips. How he managed to unlock the door and vanish so fast escaped her. Why would he do that to her in the middle of an interview? How was she supposed to go to Monica and carry on like this? What if she had worn lipstick? Was she even a little bit upset he had lied to her or rather avoided the truth about who he was? Granted, maybe he would've told her all this if she had told him anything about herself or where she went to school.

Taking the few minutes she needed to calm herself down, she adjusted her hair and clothing. Then, she stepped out of the stuffy office. She found out then there was a bathroom across the hall, and she entered, shutting the door behind her. Crossing to the expansive sink, she turned the brass faucet on and let the cool water gush over her hands, anything to turn down the heat that consumed her. Looking up, she found her makeup was, for the most part, still intact. There was a bit of her high coverage foundation rubbed off her nose, but she decided she could live with that. It had been a lucky chance today was one of the days she chose to wear irritatingly thick contact lenses instead of her tortoise-shell glasses. Those buggers could really get in the way of a good make out if you let them. She could only hope she didn't smell too much like sex.

After using the rest room, she found her way back to the front desk where she found Monica sitting with a ginormous smile on her face. "Welcome to the team!" She moved from behind the desk and engulfed Jenn in a congratulatory hug. The excitement was unreal.

She couldn't believe it. "Wait... I got the job?"

"Yes, you can start tomorrow! Your schedule will be

Monday through Friday, just come in whenever you're not at school. "

"Oh my gosh! Yay! I am so excited."

"You'll just have to let us know the night before if you won't be able to make it to work that day. The next step for you is to accept and then decide what you'd like to get paid and how often." Had she heard her correct? Why would there be any reservations on her part? The answer was yes.

"Uh, what do you mean 'decide what you'd like to get paid'?"

"The Giulianis give that opportunity to young stylists with outstanding potential through their Prodigy Program. It's kind of like a sponsorship to help you reach your own goals and relieve any anxieties you might have outside of work so you can put all of your focus into hair and into learning as much about the business as you can. We are going to set up a schedule with stylists you'll be working with each day and we'll be sending you to seminars and workshops. On top of that, any time a class is offered at a Giuliani's location, you will be welcome and highly encouraged to attend." Monica shared the information as if it were just an everyday conversation, not a conversation that would flip Jenn's world upside down.

"I-I am just a bit overwhelmed. I was expecting to maybe get paid minimum wage with the occasional tip from a client after shampooing them. This is way more than I could have ever hoped for. Doesn't it seem a bit unfair to the other stylists who have more experience and have been working here longer?"

"Don't worry about anyone else. This is about you and your future. The only people who will know how much you get paid are the Giulianis and myself, unless you choose to tell others. It's understandable that you would be overwhelmed. Just take the evening to think about it and we can talk money tomorrow when you show up for work."

"That sounds like a good idea. Thank you so much, Monica! I will see you tomorrow."

"See you tomorrow."

With Monica's encouraging wave and grin, Jenn headed towards the front door. It chimed as she opened it and she stepped out into the fresh, September air.

Jenn opened her beat up car door and ducked in. As soon as the door was shut, she began sobbing. She couldn't believe this day. Hot sex, a hot new job and a hot new salary? Who was she to be deserving of such good fortune?

Chapter 4

Jenn had been on auto pilot the entire thirty minute drive home, contemplating how she should go about the situation. Could she really accept the offer and carry on with the rest of her life? It was all too much and she got the feeling it was too good to be true. She wasn't sure she would be able to act on the offer given the circumstances. Mr. Giuliani had kissed her moments before Monica said she had officially got the job. Could she trust him not to use his position of authority against her? He would basically be supplying her with her dream income and she had to do whatever he desired of her, this wasn't something she could be okay with. Her free will was important to her. However, there was a voice in the back of her mind, telling her this could be a good thing and technically it wouldn't be his money, it'd be his family company's money, right? Mr. Giuliani could have pure intentions and her salary and career could be separate from her relationship with him, but was she naïve for hoping it? She definitely needed to know what his first name actually was. She'd also like to know if his mother had any knowledge of what her son was up to.

Turning right into the driveway of her apartment complex, Jenn appreciated the white flowers blossoming on the trees that decorated the entrance. Was she blossoming too? She parked her car in the uncovered parking spot she had become familiar with, not wanting to pay extra for a covered spot. Maybe, all of this would change. Would she outgrow this home for a new one? Jenn opened the driver's side door and with one high-heeled foot after the other, made her way to her front door, passing by the community dumpster. There was a certain pep in her step due to the thought she might potentially be able to afford to not be neighbors with a literal pile of trash.

Standing over her doormat, which was covered in lemons and said 'Hello', she turned the key in the lock and shoved the door wide open. Her roommate, Katie, was in the living room, watching Netflix while lounging on their black velvet futon and holding an entire loaf of bread in her hand. Katie had an adoration for those cheap, day old loaves of bread you can find at the grocery store deli and she often took to eating them for a snack as if they were a bunch of grapes or a bag of Doritos.

"There's something different about ya than when you left today. I'm guessing you got the job. Are you excited?" The words were formed around a piece of bread that was still in the back of her mouth. She swallowed the bite and waited for more details.

"You will not believe the crazy day I've had." She left her dress shoes by the front door and planted herself in their lumpy leather recliner, needing to kick up her tired feet for a few minutes to think.

Jenn told Katie everything from her deep conversation with Monica to her steamy quickie with Anthony to the glamorous job offering and dream salary proposition. She told her everything she had been thinking on her drive home, knowing

Katie would understand and have some sort of advice for her. Her friend always had something to say and would speak her mind. Jenn knew she would give an honest opinion even if it differed from her own. For a second, she did think about the fact she had already broken her simple promise to Mr. Giuliani to 'keep her mouth shut', but surely he wouldn't mind her telling her roommate who was a medical student and very unlikely to ever be a part of the salon crowd. Who would she have to tell?

Katie was attentive as she listened to everything Jenn had to say, asking a quick question here and there. For the most part, she just soaked the information up. Once Jenn had finished, she expected Katie to start in on her without hesitation. To her surprise, she took a while after Jenn had stopped speaking before saying anything. Perhaps, she was weighing the pros and cons of all the differing reactions swirling through her curly-haired head. This drawn out pause made Jenn more nervous than she originally thought possible.

Just when Jenn was about to say it was obviously too good to be true and she wasn't going to accept the generous offer, Katie finally broke the deafening silence.

"So, what number are you going to give them?" That wasn't at all the response Jennifer had been expecting.

"I don't even know if I'm going to agree to it yet. Don't you think it's a little weird? The unlikeliness of it all, along with Mr. Giuliani's interest in me?"

"If you're asking me if it's weird that he's into you, that's an absolute no. How could he not be into you? The rest of it, however, is far beyond a little weird. There are some things about it I don't like. If you ever piss him off, will he fire you or lower your pay? As for whether you should pursue anything romantic with the man, I think you should steer clear of him. I've been telling you that you need to stop going for dirty boys and I think he sounds like another one of those. So, there's my opinion. What are you going to tell them? Because I know you have a number picked out already. You've been saying you were gonna be a gazillionaire. I just never thought it was going to be a wealthy Italian family that'd help kick start your financial freedom."

She couldn't say she was surprised by Katie's disapproval. Katie had high standards for herself and for her friends. If she were honest with herself, she knew everything Katie had said was valid. Katie did know her better than she knew herself and she'd be lying if she said Katie was incorrect about her already having her magic number stowed away in the back of her mind. She had actually had the number for months now, saved in a spreadsheet on her computer. It was important for her to be specific about her goals, so she had made herself a dream budget as something to reach for. Now, she could have it with barely any effort.

As she ruminated, she came to the realization of what she needed and wanted before moving on with her decision: a word with Mr. Giuliani. Jenn needed to know his intentions. She had to be sure she was really qualified for the program and not chosen due to his desire for her. Was she going to feel like she was living off a man instead of providing for herself on her own? Even though, technically, it was payment for her real job.

"What would you think if I called their office and asked if I could have a word with Mr. Giuliani? Maybe drive up there and confront him in person?" Jenn looked to her friend. To say Katie's opinion was important to her would be an understatement.

"I don't think that's a good idea. I think you should cut him off. You can take the job but keep your relationship with him professional. If you go see him alone at his office, you're just going to give in and have sex with him. I mean, are you his girlfriend? Are you his pet? Are you friends with benefits? You need to know what this really is."

"I know you're right and I would much rather have this job than him and having him will jeopardize my job in the long run, but I still feel like I need to communicate all of this to him in person."

"All right… if that's what you think you need, I'll drive you there. We can stop and get champagne to celebrate on the way home."

"Champagne for what?" Jenn asked.

"Who cares that you're not going to have him? We need to celebrate you being selected for this program and you getting the job!"

"Oh, do you think I should be drinking tonight? I mean, I will be having my first day on the job tomorrow. I want to leave a good impression."

Katie's face scrunched up like it did when she saw someone doing something ridiculous in public, a mix of humor and irritation. "Don't be ridiculous. It's just champagne. You could have three glasses and you'd be fine for work tomorrow."

On the drive over, Jennifer called the perky receptionist at the Giuliani business office to make sure that Mr. Giuliani was actually there. She also used the time to touch up her makeup, looking into the passenger visor mirror. She was pleasantly surprised to see her tears had barely caused a shift in her appearance. Thank God for 24-hour make-up.

Nervous, but feeling more confident than she had in a while, Jenn stepped out of Katie's suburban onto the concrete sidewalk that led up to the office building. Upon opening the business door, she found the receptionist she had now spoken to twice. The young woman fit her voice. A tiny, little thing in a lemon-yellow sundress with matching baby pink nails and lipstick. Jenn wondered why Anthony didn't just make a move on his front desk clerk, she was cute enough. How did she know he hadn't already and who was she to be thinking all jealous like this? She had seen him a total of three times!

"Welcome to Giuliani's. You must be Jennifer." Had Jenn said her name over the phone? She didn't think she did.

"I am, how do you know my name already?" She attempted to hide her tone, revealing how weirded out she truly was. She hoped she didn't sound too rude.

"Mr. Giuliani informed me this afternoon that a young, pretty girl named Jennifer would be stopping by to see him. I received your phone call inquiring about his whereabouts. Then, a young and pretty girl comes through the door about thirty minutes after the call. I took my chances and connected the dots." The girl was a bit ramble-y and awkward, but in an endearing way. When exactly had Mr. Giuliani alerted her of Jenn's arrival? She said the afternoon, but Jenn had only decided she would come see him about an hour ago and it was now seven o' clock How had he known she was coming?

"Let me get you a water before you head back." The girl disappeared into a backroom a few yards away and returned promptly, holding a bottle of artisan water, glass container and everything. Sure, she hadn't been offered the option of bubbly or flat, but she was still impressed.

Jenn offered her thanks and accepted the water, thankful because she knew being around Mr. Giuliani would render her super thirsty.

"Er- this seems silly to ask at this point, but… what's Mr. Giuliani's first name?" Sure, Jenn was embarrassed to have to ask, but he was already one step ahead of her, knowing she would stop by. She had to have something on him.

"I sure do hope we've been referring to the right Giuliani

this whole time and not his brother or father. I kind of just assumed which is completely my fault. I believe you're here to see Anthony. If not, I am so sorry. The other two Mr. Giulianis are no longer here and you'll have to reschedule."

"Well, let's just cross our fingers we've got the right one today."

"You can head down the hall. Last door on the left. He'll be waiting for you. Good luck!" Had the receptionist just given her a cheeky wink or was Jenn having a stroke? Does the girl know something Jenn doesn't? Was she the one girl of many to come calling on Anthony Giuliani? Granted, it could have just been a friendly gesture. The receptionist did give off the vibe that she probably winks at people often. It probably had been nothing and Jenn was reading too much into it.

Should she knock or enter without warning? She had been a bit irritated that he already knew she was coming. She had wanted to catch him off guard, so she decided against knocking. Mainly to help her feel like she somewhat still had some level of control over the situation.

The rest of what she'd seen of the building was the usual, boring office setup. Stepping into Anthony's office was quite a dramatic shift. It looked as if it could be the oval office. He had a large, oak, executive desk he was seated behind. There were books and taxidermy animals and brown leather seating. The room even smelled like raw manliness, looking around Jennifer realized there were no candles or aroma-enhancing paraphernalia. The smell was the result of housing Anthony over the past few years. She didn't know if it was his aftershave or his shampoo or just his natural pheromones, but it worked well in his favor. It just added to the overall sexiness of the Italian. He truly was any woman's dream. Any woman in her right mind at least.

Jenn had expected him to jump or be startled by her entrance or even short and rude because of her intruding, but she received nothing. He just continued reading the paper-work laid out in front of him. Without looking up, he instructed her, "Take a seat."

Not wanting trouble, she did as she was told. What should she say? She felt like he should lead the conversation as he somehow knew she was coming before she had. He should at least explain himself. She shouldn't have to ask.

Neither of them broke the silence. Jenn looking at Anthony, Anthony looking at his paperwork. She knew she should be irritated. Wasn't Anthony being a bit rude? However, she wasn't bothered. In fact, she was into it. Neither of them had to say anything to send the tension in the room soaring. Katie could probably feel it all the way out in the parking lot, waiting in her car.

Jennifer cleared her throat, realizing he wasn't going to speak, when he cut her off before she had the chance to open her mouth.

"I knew you would be visiting me tonight. What can I help you with, darling?" He was still not giving her the satisfaction of a glance, but the warmth in how he had said 'darling' had her blood rushing.

"Erm, about that… how did you know I would be coming?" She couldn't help feeling embarrassed around him. She wanted to seem sophisticated, but here she was stuttering over her words and unaware what the other party knew or what information he had access to that she hadn't.

"It would be unrealistic for me to think, after such great sex, you wouldn't be coming back for more." With the laddish comment, he finally sneaked a peek at her. His eyes flickering with amusement as he smirked. You could tell he felt quite proud of himself.

"Actually, that isn't why I'm here." Finally, she had the upper hand. If he really thought she would call and inquire about him, hunt him down, and make the drive for another round, he would be brutally mistaken. The arrogance of the man. Feeling herself getting heated, she went in with everything that was concerning her. Mentioning the money, whether or not she believed it was a real program or not, and that she wasn't the type of girl to accept money from a man, at least not so much money.

"First of all, missy, let me invite you to get off your high horse. You have no need to get all hot and bothered over me." He added a wink. "You'll learn, in future, any woman who speaks to me with that tone will receive the application of my hand to her behind."

Her ears weren't enough to hold the hotness rushing to her head, her cheeks inflamed, and she felt like she might explode.

"Secondly, it is a real program and I have nothing to do with it. I was shocked when you called and I apologize for hanging up on you, but I had to take the time to figure out how I felt about the strange coincidence. I do not need to offer any sort of compensation in order to find a woman to engage with me romantically. As you should remember, I did manage to get you into my bed before all this. Only desperate men spend their money in that way. Is it your intention to call me desperate?"

Jenn shook her head, looking at the flooring and wanting to cry. She was embarrassed. Had she been behaving childishly?

"I would like to hear you say it, Ms. Caman."

"No."

"No, what?"

"No, I do not think you are desperate."

"You'll learn to add sir to your responses in time, but now that that's settled, and we are clear that I'm not in desperate need of you. I will let you know the program typically has some guidelines. You'd show a budget, detailing how you would be spending the money each month, and there would be certain limitations-

"That's no problem! I actually have a budget already that I can show you. And I-"

"Did I say I was finished explaining? I was about to say that is the norm, but you are not the norm and will be getting paid each month directly from my account so there will not be the usual limitations."

"No limitations?"

"No, within reason, of course."

"Does your mother know this is how I'll be getting paid? Are you only doing this because we had sex?"

"Though my mother runs the Prodigy Program, she doesn't handle finances or payroll. You and I are the only ones who will know of the arrangement. I have found women are more likely to surrender control in the bedroom when they feel they are in control of their finances and careers. I do plan to pursue you romantically, but that isn't why I've chosen to do this. I'm doing this because I want to. I am not obligated to give you any more of an explanation."

"If I didn't want to be pursued by you romantically, would you still be making this offer?"

"If that were the case, I'd still make the offer, but we know that's not the case. However, you should know my approach towards relationships isn't the usual, it's much kinkier as you've seen from my closet, and if that makes you uncomfortable at all, you should let me know now." Those green eyes were at it again, piercing into her soul and making her squirm. She knew she should call it off like Katie said, but she was already wet between her thighs.

"No…"

"No, what?"

Smirking, she said it at last and she was proud of herself for not cringing. "No, sir."

"Good girl, now what'll it be?" He was logging onto his computer as if he were about to deposit the money then and there. Should she be reasonable and lower her price or should she go with her gut and be honest? What if he thought she was out of her mind? She could always pretend she was joking depending on his response. What if her answer was too low and it came as a slap in the face, as if she thought he didn't have enough money? She gave him her original dream number, confident as she spoke the answer aloud.

His reaction was the sexiest thing she'd experienced of him yet. He didn't flinch. He didn't even flutter an eyelash. It was as if she were the most reasonable and sound-minded person on earth. Admiring his Patek Philippe watch, she realized his reaction must be fitting for a business mogul of his caliber.

"All right, and how would you like to receive it? Weekly? Bi-weekly? Monthly? It's all up to you."

"Monthly."

"Last question, what day would you like to be paid each month?"

At this point, she was already feeling much more comfortable around him and was ready to start letting her real personality shine through. Besides, she should be partying it up right now. She was on cloud nine.

"Hmmm. What's today?"

She couldn't believe it. She had gotten a laugh out of him, looked like he could let loose a bit after all. The Mr. Tough Guy act was getting old and if she were being honest, she couldn't be with someone who was always serious. Sure, that was hot and all, but she needed some contrast to break it up and really make her appreciate his stern manliness.

"Uh- I believe it's the 15th." Glancing at his calendar, he confirmed, "Yeah, it's the 15th."

"How about the 16th of every month, then?" She couldn't

help giggling. She was so excited. What would be the first thing she did when she got paid? Pay her bills and rent? Maybe. Buy new shoes for her new job? Definitely. Buy new lace to impress her Italian? For sure.

He was enraptured. She was the cutest thing he had ever laid eyes on. Her personality was the perfect mix of sass and accommodation. She knew how to listen when she needed to, but she also had made him laugh. Most women couldn't do that. They usually just irritated him and here he was, having a connection with a young girl who was just excited to be doing hair and getting paid good money for it. Women his age were not like this. Had her answer shocked him? One-hundred percent. Would he let her know that? Not in a million years. He had a feeling she was well worth it and she would put the money to good use. It was an easy decision for him.

"I'm letting you know that's definitely not something we would do for every prodigy, but for you, I'll make an exception. We do have a contract you'll need to take home, review, and sign. The first part is like any other prodigy's, but at the end, I had my lawyer write up an agreement for us both to keep your salary and our relationship separate. You'll see I have already signed. Give the front part to Monica tomorrow, and the second part to me on Friday night. Now, I am going to set up an appointment for you to meet up with one of my fiduciaries in a few months. I want you to be set up to succeed on your way to financial freedom. Of course, you can always come to me if you need it, but he will be a great help to you."

What the fuck is a fiduciary? Jennifer had no idea, but she

figured she didn't need to know just now, seeing as the meeting would be in a few months. Now, that business had been settled, would she get more of what she had tasted earlier? She had her fingers crossed.

"You need to cut it out with those bedroom eyes, little girl. As much as I'd like to bend you over my desk and rip that all too-tight skirt off you, I'm not going to do anything like that with you tonight to further show you our intimate relationship is separate from our business relationship. Also, I think it'll be best for you if you don't speak of our intimate relationship with any classmates or coworkers. Now leave my office before I change my mind about fucking you."

Disappointed, but anxious to get back to Katie and tell her everything, – beside the fact she didn't call it off with Anthony – Jennifer got up and headed out. Passing by the front desk, there was no sign of the yellow sundress, and she figured the receptionist had already headed home. Hopefully, Katie wouldn't be irritated she had been in there so long. Granted, if she and Anthony had let their more carnal desires out, she would've been in there much longer.

As she opened the door, she found Katie wasn't angry, but eager to hear what had happened. "So? Did you fuck?"

"Er, no, but we got everything else sorted. My payroll has been set up."

"Cool, so where are we buying the champagne then?"

"Bitch, we're not just getting champagne. We're going out for steaks and lobster and caviar."

Chapter 5

Jennifer Caman woke Tuesday morning bright and early. It felt like her life had always been leading up to this, preparing her.

She began making her bed. She had never been the type to make her bed before and there wasn't much to make as she only had one pillow and a couple of throws. She also only had one blanket, that wasn't big enough for her queen, and no top sheet, so it wasn't the most beautifully made bed either. She longed to be curled up in Anthony's bed, with his silk sheets and down comforter.

Jenn left her room, heading for the shower. She was tiptoeing and turning door handles as slowly as possible, trying to be quiet because she knew Katie wouldn't want to be waking up for a couple more hours. Entering the bathroom, she began stripping off her matching pajama set. Both the tops and bottoms were leopard print and lined with black lace. What did Anthony wear to bed when she wasn't with him? Did he just sleep naked or did he wear some sort of lush pajamas? Pajamas weren't always the most flattering things for men to wear and Jenn couldn't even imagine what a man with money might wear to bed, but she could guess it wasn't fleece pajama pants covered in the 'Mtn. Dew' symbol as one of her exes had worn.

Standing under her waterfall showerhead, Jennifer prepared herself. She had heard somewhere that it was a good habit to begin your morning with a freezing cold shower. Jenn was a baby, however, and didn't endure the entire shower with cold water. She would stand in the icy downpour for thirty seconds and then reward herself with much appreciated warmth. Did Anthony have any weird rituals he did in the morning? Was he a morning person? Jenn had read a lot of books and watched a ton of videos on habits of the world's millionaires and some of them had pretty 'out there' routines. How crazy would it be if he did cold showers too?

The fruity smell of Jennifer's shampoo engulfed the steam as she pumped the liquid into her hand, a glop as big as a ping pong ball. She may be cheap when it came to bedding, but any self-respecting beauty guru couldn't just use drugstore products. This particular line was supposed to make your hair grow. Sure, Jenn already had beautiful hair that reached past her nipples, but a girl can always want more. She wouldn't be satisfied till the ends were at the middle of her back. Come to think of it, she might be in the market for some extensions, given she had the income for it now. It would only help to enhance her personal image as a stylist, and more hair for Anthony to pull couldn't hurt either.

After rinsing both the shampoo and conditioner from her hair, she took to lathering her loofa up with body wash, hints of rose and lavender enveloping her senses. She was thorough in the care of herself and made sure every bit and crevice of her had been accounted for as she glided over her smooth, pale skin. She was thinking about Anthony… again and what it would be like to take a shower with him. Was he the sort to be into shower sex? Or would it be romantic, with him doing the lathering for her and she for him in return? Would he pump those manly fingers into her or would he push her to her knees, commanding her to blow him with water pouring over her face as she did so?

She switched the flow of water from the rainfall head that was connected to the ceiling above her to the detachable shower head, laying with her back on the bottom of the tub. She had her right leg up and near her head, resting it on the shelf that usually would hold a bar of soap. Her left leg remaining outstretched, she directed the showerhead at the center of her arousal, visions of Anthony motivating her every move. The pressure was high. It didn't take long for her to be nearing her peak. She imagined watching Anthony's trapezius muscles stretching and pulling, in a mirror behind them, as he thrust into her again and again, not trying to be gentle for a minute. She climaxed with a satisfied smile on her face. Would Anthony have felt the need to punish her for finishing without permission? Jennifer had never been spanked before, but the thought of it made her blood race and to receive a spanking from someone as sexy and powerful as Anthony would surely send her over the edge.

Jenn was careful as she stepped out of the shower, her legs a little shaky. Grabbing one of her pink towels from the hook on the wall and wrapping her hair, she was thankful to have had a little bit of 'me time' before beginning her busy day. However, she wasn't completely satisfied as she was eager and a little bit desperate for the real thing.

How would a woman who has a great job and a banging man, dress? After looking into a couple of drawers in her tall emerald-painted dresser, she gave up and turned to check her closet. Opening the collapsible doors, she sighed. There wasn't much there for her either. She would definitely need to go on a little shopping spree to buy some more professional looking clothes. A bit dejectedly she decided on a plain, black dress that fell just below her knees. It had short sleeves and looked like it had shoulder pads, even though it didn't. It was a plain, stiff untextured material besides a little ruffle at the bottom that was satin. She paired the look with her Doc Martens booties that were also all black. She would've liked to have worn heels, but thought better of it because it would be a long day.

Grabbing her large Michael Kors purse her mom had given her last Christmas, her coffee, her keys, and wheeling her hair case behind her, she left the small apartment. Careful not to spill her coffee onto her pretty dress, she made her way to her Buick.

Arriving at Giuliani's, Jenn did feel a bit of nerves. Before heading in, she took a moment to reapply her lip-gloss and to give herself a pep talk. Feeling as good as possible, she left the car and headed for her destiny.

———

Monica was at the entrance, clearly waiting for Jennifer's arrival. Opening the door for her, she greeted Jenn with a peppy good morning. This was a good sign. The last place Jennifer worked had been a horrible experience and the majority of the issues could be directed towards her being the only morning person. So she was happy to be alive? Sue her. She didn't see the need to be grumpy and cold for the first few hours of the morning just because she was sleepy. It didn't make sense to her. They could drink some coffee and get over themselves, in her opinion.

"Hey, Jenn! Are you excited for your first day? I know we all are happy to have you join our team. I'm sure you noticed all the curious glances your way yesterday. It always gets the creative juices flowing in the building when somebody new joins."

"Hey! Yes! I'm super excited. It's going to be great."

Monica led her to the front desk where there was some paperwork waiting for them.

"So Mr. Giuliani has already been in today and let me know you're already set up for payroll. That's great. I'm proud of you for making that decision for yourself and it means one less thing we have to go over before I can introduce you to your stylist for the week. I think you're going to really enjoy learning from her. I went with someone based on some of the services you said you most enjoyed doing." Monica talked really fast, but it wasn't in a way that implied she was rushing their conversation and wanted to get on with the rest of her day. It seemed as if she were truly excited for Jenn. She was flipping through the stack of papers, discarding the irrelevant documents and placing the ones she needed aside. When she was finished, there were only about five forms that needed to be filled out. Easy stuff: Giuliani's mission statement, code of conduct, dress code and such, the basic staffing matters.

Attaching the papers to a brown corkboard clipboard and handing Jenn a ballpoint pen, with 'Giulianis' imprinted across it, Monica left her to fill out the pages without her chirping excitedly in her ear. Obviously, she wanted Jenn to hurry because she was so excited to have her meet her stylist. Jenn hoped they would get along and she would be able to learn something new today, even if it was something small. Monica also said she'd bring Jenn a bubbly when she came back which was nice, considering she had remembered her preference from the day before.

As she sat there initialing, signing and filling out the usual information –address, phone number, etc. – one of the stylists couldn't wait for Monica to introduce Jenn to the team and came and introduced himself. His name was Mikey and he had tight leather pants, tattoos and a hoop through his septum, but a goofy grin and small friendly voice, which were a strong contradiction to his appearance. Feeling welcomed and admired, Jenn said hello. She knew he wouldn't be the stylist she would train with this week. But she could always train with him in the future, she supposed.

Jennifer had been finished with the paperwork for a few minutes before Monica returned with the Perrier. Taking the glass bottle from the woman's perfectly manicured hand, with a thank you, Jenn unscrewed the cap and took a swig, thankful for the drink but hoping the bubbles didn't give her the urge to burp.

"Here is the signed Prodigy Program contract packet too."

"Perfect, thank you. Okay, Jenn! If you'll follow me, I'll introduce you to your stylist and you can get your day started. You're going to have so much fun with her."

Her? Hmmm, so that told Jenn it definitely wasn't Mikey.

"Remind me again, what time are you leaving for school today?" Monica asked.

"I have to leave at noon to have time to grab lunch before arriving at school at one."

"Perfect, just let Maybella know."

Maybella? Would she be as unique as her name? Jenn, crossed her fingers hoping it was a yes. The more unique the stylist the better.

Passing by the spiral staircase, Monica guided her across the salon floor. Heads turned of both client and staff alike. Jenn hoped it was because they found her intriguing or pretty and not because of something embarrassing like having toothpaste on her black dress. Glancing down, there wasn't any gunk of the toothpaste variety anywhere on her, but that didn't rule out there being something weird on her face or her hair sticking up funny. Jenn reached up and smoothed her hair before tossing it over her shoulder.

They reached the far corner of the room. It was as if Monica had taken Jenn on a 'fresh meat' parade. She felt like they were sizing her up. Did any of them know about what had happened with Anthony in the office yesterday? Or did they know how much she was getting paid? Or did they know she was only a third of her way through her cosmetology program and shouldn't have been given this opportunity?

"Jennifer, this is Maybella. She was the first to shoot her hand up when I asked the staff which of them would like to work with you first. I think you two will really get along so I'm going to get out of both of your hair, so you can both get into some hair, if you know what I mean. If you need anything, Jenn, just find me and ask. I'm here for you." She gently pushed Jenn towards Maybella, coercing the two into getting to know each other.

Jennifer thought Maybella was going to go for a handshake, but she lunged in for a familial hug, whispering in Jenn's ear, "Just so you know... I know about you and Anthony. Don't piss me off or I will make sure everyone knows: the staff at all four locations, your educators, your classmates, and all of the Giulianis."

After making the comment, her new trainer smiled brightly as if she had never said anything. Jenn thought it best not to react... she had no idea what to say and honestly? Maybella had definitely gotten to her.

"Well, like she said, I'm Maybella. I cannot tell you just how excited I am about you joining our team." The woman was very petite. If she hadn't been wearing the tall lace-up boots with huge heels, she would've been much shorter than Jenn which was saying something because Jenn was short herself. She was wearing acid-washed jeans with slits in the knees and a flowy black top, matching her boots. She had short, staggered layers of curly, fiery red hair. To a layman, she would have seemed to be a natural redhead since her eyebrows and her pale skin fit the stereotype, but Jenn had a feeling it had taken a lot of work for her to get her hair like that. Were her curls real?

"Monica told us you're interested in specializing in textured hair and blondes, which was why I was so excited to have you work with me because textured hair is kind of my thing. I can't say I have the most expertise in blondes out of our whole team, but I think I can still offer you some useful information. And you're gonna be able to work with other stylists in the future, so I'm sure you'll learn everything you're hoping to."

The day went by quickly and she did enjoy herself. She kept wishing the whisper from Maybella had never happened but she knew it had, and it made her feel like she had just signed a contract agreeing to her social and career suicide.

Chapter 6

It had been a long week of learning and hustling to and from the salon and school. She loved her new job. It kept her so busy she barely had time to sit and obsess over Maybella's threat, how she knew about her and Anthony, or what she should do about it. Now that she was home for the weekend, those racing thoughts wouldn't stop. It was Friday and Anthony had said he would see her tonight, but she hadn't heard anything from him since, so she assumed he had forgotten. Which was good, because now she wouldn't have to come up with an excuse as to why she didn't want to see him. The only way she could exercise some sort of control over the Maybella situation was by never seeing Anthony again.

On her way home today, she stopped to pick up a pizza, a bottle of wine, and a face mask. She was prepared for an evening of relaxing and watching old episodes of *Sex & The City*. This was all a front for what she was really doing underneath her calm appearance: not allowing herself a second to think about Anthony and his six-pack.

She was thankful Katie would be gone for the weekend

because that meant Jenn could really chill and not have to think about cleaning or turning her music down. Typically, she holed herself up in her room, tucked into bed with Netflix, but tonight was a night that should be spent in the living room with the good TV. Was she totally lame for just wanting to be alone in her apartment? She did have the money to take herself out now with no worries if she wanted, but it just sounded exhausting at this point. Maybe, tomorrow she would go to the mall and spa or something.

She had just switched into comfy clothes and had released her boobs from boob jail – aka her bra – when someone started pounding on her front door. Who could possibly be here? She hadn't ordered her pizza, she had it already and was just about to take her first bite. It couldn't be her neighbors asking that she please turn her TV down because she hadn't even turned it on yet. Could she just pretend she wasn't home like you do when Jehovah's Witnesses come by?

The knocking continued, persistent. With a resigned sigh, she kicked her recliner back into place and got up. As she opened the door, she crossed her arms over her chest in an attempt to hide the fact she was without a bra. Standing outside was an older gentleman in a black and white suit. She had never seen this man before. Who the hell was he and why was he dressed like he was stopping by the Queen's palace once he was done here?

"Hello, Miss. Mr. Giuliani sent me to pick you up. He said you should be waiting for me?" As he made the comment, his eyes scanned Jenn head to toe. It wasn't in a disdainful way, but in a way that said, 'Sorry, I clearly am at the wrong apartment'.

So Anthony had a personal chauffeur, one who dressed like a mid-century butler. Who did this Giuliani think he was to just assume she would be waiting for him? He had never communicated actual plans with her. He had only made a passing comment. No. The hell if he thought she would just come the moment he beckoned.

"I'm sorry, sir. Anthony never spoke to me about a date this evening and he never told me you would be coming. I'm sorry you had to drive all this way, but I won't be going out tonight."

The chauffeur's mouth opened and closed a couple of times, making it obvious he was dumbfounded.

"I'm sorry, miss, but you have to come with me. Mr. Giuliani will not be pleased if I come back and you aren't with me."

She couldn't say she wasn't curious about what Anthony had planned for them, but her pride wouldn't allow it. She would refuse to go simply on principle. Hopefully, Anthony didn't take it out on the driver too badly. Even if she wanted to, she couldn't go out now. She was not dressed for it. Her hair and makeup would both need to be done and she had no idea what she would wear.

"I'm sorry, but you'll just have to tell Anthony to deal with it."

And with that, Jenn shut the door in the man's face. She partially felt bad, but she could tell this man absolutely would not leave if she continued her nice act. He forced her hand.

About an hour later and about three of Samantha's sexcapades into her show, there was another knock at the door. Who the hell could that be now? Who drops by unannounced on a Friday around dinner time? Honestly, it's just bad manners. This time, she really wasn't going to answer. She wasn't home.

Five minutes passed and there was still knocking. Why couldn't they take a hint? Before yanking the door open and telling this person off, she looked through the peephole and there he was: Anthony Giuliani.

"Jennifer Caman, open this door right now. I know you're

home." He looked angry and the fact he was yelling through her door at her wasn't a good sign either. No matter how much she pretended, she didn't really want to avoid him and seeing him looking so upset wasn't fun either. I mean, all she had to do was make a point to not piss Maybella off and they'd be fine, right?

With reluctance, she opened the door and he immediately shoved past her into the apartment. He went to the couch and sat down in the middle of it, his arms crossed, facing towards her as she closed the front door.

"What's going on, Jennifer? Gerard didn't deserve for you to shut the door in his face and I told you I'd see you on Friday. I don't understand what the problem is. Are you trying to be a brat?"

He didn't look happy. That's all she could think and the rage and disappointment in his eyes just about shattered her. She was already on the verge of tears, but she knew she couldn't be mad at him. He had no idea of Maybella's threats.

"I-I'm… I don't know what to say. You never really confirmed we would be going out tonight, you just said it in a passing comment. I didn't know you really meant it. I was upset you expected me to come without a call, first." Even as the words were leaving her mouth, she realized how childish they were. Anthony was a grown man. He was too old to be playing those sorts of games with her. She was embarrassed by her stubbornness.

"You need to learn this. If I say something, I mean it. I don't make passing comments. Things aren't maybes with me. So you're upset with me, why be rude to my driver? Now, he has had to drive from my place to yours, then back to get me, and now back again. You're going to apologize. Do you hear me?"

Jenn could feel her lip quivering, but she couldn't let herself cry. Her weak reply, "Yes," gave her away.

"Yes, what?"

"Yes, sir."

"Now, I can't just let this slide, darling. I think you know you should be disciplined for this." At the word 'disciplined', he was already rolling up his sleeves.

Jenn didn't think she could handle being spanked for the first time right now. She already felt bad enough as it was, but she couldn't form the words and she found herself walking towards him.

"Come on, now. Over my lap. That's it."

Maybe, she could handle it. As she bent over his lap, he gently brushed her hair over her shoulder and slid her shorts and panties to her ankles. Then again, how gentle could he be with his huge hands? She was thankful to be looking at the floor where he couldn't see her face because one loose tear got away and hit the fluffy rug beneath.

Anthony was rubbing her ass cheeks and gave a gentle squeeze as he said, "Do you still want your safe word to be 'apricots'?"

She nodded her head, not wanting to speak because her voice would show how upset she was.

"I want to hear you say it."

"Yes, sir." The words were covered by the sound of his hand smacking into the center of her bouncy booty cheeks and by her letting out her first scream of many. She tried to roll off the side of his lap and get away, but he only held her tighter. After just a few spanks, her ass was already tingly and hot. She managed to stop screaming with every swat, but now she was sobbing, ugly blubbering sobbing, and she was mortified. She felt so stupid. She wished she had just gone with Gerard the first time.

Anthony began to lighten up and the sound of Jenn crying became the most prominent sound in the room, louder than the sound of his hand meeting her bottom. She thought it was just about over. He was gripping her ass with his bare hand and had stopped punishing her. Just when she attempted to stand up, he pushed her back down and began spanking her behind faster than he had before. These spanks weren't as harsh but because she was already tender, it seemed much worse.

Jennifer was completely and totally exhausted. She wanted to get away from Anthony and never have to look at him again. He delivered one last resounding wallop and allowed her to remove herself from him.

She wanted to run, but she was too tired from crying and from pain. She sank to the floor, sobbing. Her chest hurt and she felt like she couldn't catch enough breath. She was in a full-blown panic, but was already pushed too far to try and calm down in order to save herself the embarrassment of having him see her like this.

Anthony moved as if to scoop her into his arms. This broke her out of the moment as she got to her feet. She grabbed her shorts and panties and ran to the bathroom and locked the door behind her.

"Jennifer, you need to come out and talk to me. Now." His tone was firm, but with the undertone of concern.

"No, Anthony! *I hate you!* Go away!" She couldn't stop her tears. They were relentless and she truly felt they would never stop. She just wanted to be alone and to never have to talk to him or look at him again.

"I understand you're upset, Jenn, and since this is your first spanking, I will ignore your outburst. However, I'm going to be right outside this door until you calm down and are ready to come out and talk to me about it."

She heard him slide down the other side of the door. His voice was so near. The worry in his voice softened her to him a little bit and her thoughts began to slow and become clearer.

She knew in her core he wasn't going to leave, and even though she hadn't liked the spanking at all, him staying even after she told him to leave meant a lot.

She opened the door and she couldn't help the giggle that came out. Anthony had been leaning so heavily against the door, he moved backwards a bit once the support was gone. He even cracked a smile.

"Come here." He was still seated on the floor, but had his arms wide, inviting her in. She fell into his arms, still naked from the waist down as she set on his lap. He hugged her close, breaking the seal of tears open again, squeezing her as she cried into his shoulder.

He waited for her to settle a bit and pull away from his shoulder before speaking. "You took your first spanking very well, my dear. I'm proud of you. Don't push me out, though. Talk to me. Are you upset with me about anything else, besides the spanking, which was earned?" he said, with apparent concern on his face.

She thought she'd be afraid of him after the spanking, but his eyes were so kind. He was easy to talk to and all of her thoughts and worries came falling free. She didn't feel judged but supported. It felt as if, for the first time, someone was giving her one-hundred percent of their attention. She told him everything that had happened at the salon that week, saving what Maybella had said for last. She was so worried he would be more upset, that he would call everything off in a desperate attempt to save his reputation, but it seemed it was nothing to him. She also confronted him about lying about his name when they first met.

"I will take care of Maybella. Don't you worry about that woman for a second. She's all bark and no bite. As for why I lied about my name, I have typically used a fake name with all my play partners in the past to separate my kink life from my professional life. However, you are a different story, I don't want you as just a play partner. Now, I will completely understand if you're really not feeling up for it, but I did have an amazing evening planned for us and have been looking forward to it all week. What do you think?"

Her heart lurched. She wanted to say yes. She did usually love surprises and she wanted to see just how much of a romantic her Italian could be, but look at her. She couldn't go out like this. She still had tears and snot on her face and what do you wear on a date with Anthony Giuliani? Surely, not jeans and a blouse.

"Anthony… look at me. I'm not dressed for a night out. I'm still half-naked!"

His face broke into a smile and he jumped up, holding her hand to bring her to her feet as well.

"I have everything figured out. Put on some comfortable pants and just follow me."

The ride to Anthony's house had felt like a dream, the two of them cuddled into the backseat of his Maybach. Classical French music played through the speakers. Could Anthony even speak French? She didn't care. What was a fifteen minute ride felt like just seconds.

Once inside his loft, he left her planted on the lush ottoman he had at the center of his living room. It looked like it was covered in bear fur or something else that was manly like that. It was cute to see such a serious businessman so giddy about the surprise he had for her. It gave her the permission she needed to relax around him and fully be herself. It didn't have to be discipline and demands all the time.

Just as Jenn was starting to get antsy, entangling and detangling her little hands into the fur, Anthony rounded the corner from the dark hallway with two of the most gorgeous women Jenn had ever seen in her life. Were they models? How was this a good surprise? Were they supposed to, like, have an orgy or something?

"Jennifer Caman, I would like to introduce to you, Polina and Miyuki, your personal hair stylist and makeup artist for the evening!"

The two women were total opposites, but both equally striking. Polina had long, slender legs – actually, everything about her was long and slender come to think of it – long sleek blonde hair, slim facial structure, and torso. She wore an elegant black dress with iridescent silver leather boots. The absence of color in her outfit and hair served to emphasize the brilliant blue of her eyes. Miyuki was petite and curvy. She stood at least a foot short of Polina's six feet. She wore tapered pants in a pattern that can only be seen and not described. Every color imaginable was present. These were paired with a plain top with ginormous puffed sleeves and high top sneakers.

It was becoming a theme. Anthony somehow always knew exactly what she needed and wanted, other than that spanking of course. She had always dreamt of being able to spend evenings just like this. I mean, who was she to have her very own styling team? After tonight, she could die happy.

Both girls had their own roller cases, Polina's black and Miyuki's pink. They didn't waste any time setting up a workspace in the living room, whipping out folding tables and ring lights. Miyuki had a beautiful assortment of makeup brushes, each one pink and studded with a singular crystal. As she moved to create the look on Jenn, she daintily held each brush as if she were painting a Mona Lisa, pinky up and everything. Polina quickly pulled the elastic band from Jenn's hair, running a brush through it and spraying at least three different products into her thick tresses. There were rollers and pins and curling irons galore. Magic was happening. Jenn didn't have to move a muscle; everything was happening around her and for her. As she sat, Gerard brought her a champagne flute and bottle of prosecco and began pouring. Where had Anthony gone?

It was a whirlwind. Neither guru took the time to speak, but not in a rude way. They were just eager to deliver the best service possible in the most efficient amount of time. Jenn would usually have wanted to give input, but the team had such an air of style about them that Jenn gave her full trust to their artistic direction of the look.

Time flew by and for once, Jenn didn't feel a headache or exhaustion from worrisome thoughts. Her mind was completely at ease. You could say she was in her bliss.

How the team managed to finish at exactly the same time was a mystery. The two were in sync as if they had been working together for many years. Neither one said a word, but stepped back in unison to take in the full picture. After a few seconds that made Jenn feel squeamish, they both sighed.

Polina clasped her hands under her chin and exclaimed, "Oh, Meez Jenn! Zees look is vonderful for you! You look beee-yooo-tiful!"

Miyuki scurried about, bending over to pull one last thing out of her pink treasure chest. Standing up, she had retracted a small handheld mirror and was holding it out for Jennifer to take a look at herself in.

"Do you like, Miss Jennifer? What you think?"

The excitement on the two girls' faces was all Jenn could pay any attention to. She hadn't even looked into the mirror yet, but now seeing as she had no choice, she looked. She half expected to disapprove of what she saw, only because the two stylists didn't know her or her style or her insecurities, but that wasn't the case. It was like seeing herself for the first time. She always knew she was beautiful, but she never thought this much. She thought of herself as a strong seven, an eight on a really good hair day. However, today she was a ten and if she could be ranked any higher than that, she would be. What would Anthony think?

Peering into the mirror, which was still held by Miyuki, Jennifer soaked up every detail and feature. Her dark hair was styled into voluminous curls, each one a work of art in itself. The front whooshed from a deep side part, swooping across her face. This made the look go from your everyday curls to vintage, Hollywood glamour. Joan Crawford couldn't hold a candle to her.

She was glowing in the dim, warm light of the living room chandelier. Her skin was luminous and dewy and drew attention, centering in on her eyes, which were painted in a gunmetal gray and smoked out with a pop of blue eyeliner. Her bushy brows were combed up and out, with gel holding them in place. They complemented her hair and framed her eyes. As for blush and bronzer, Miyuki had left this light, which gave her a girlish and youthful appearance. This only helped to enhance her seeming innocence. The look was finished off with a light, pale, pink lip shade.

"Polina! Miyuki! You have outdone yourselves. I look like a beauty queen. Thank you so much, seriously." Jennifer flung her arms around the two girls, pulling them in for a group hug.

As she pulled away, Polina replied, "You are so velcome, Meez Jennifer!" Heading towards the hallway that Anthony had disappeared into, Polina shouted, "Meester Giuliani, your lady eez veady for you!"

Anthony came out from the hallway and stepped toward the girls, slipping each a wad of bills.

"Thank you, ladies. You are much appreciated. You are free to head out whenever you're ready."

"Yes, Mr. Giuliani," the two girls said in unison, each one with their own accent, quickly moving to begin cleanup.

Anthony crossed the room to Jennifer, holding her by both shoulders and sliding down to rest with his palms clinging to her arms.

"You look ravishing, my little peach. Are you pleased?"

"Oh, yes. Thank you, sir."

"Ready to head out then?" Anthony had the biggest smile on his face. Was he teasing her?

Looking down to her comfy clothes, she couldn't tell if he really thought it was okay for her to go out like this. She didn't need to voice her concerns, though.

"I'm only kidding, peach. Follow me."

Taking her delicate hand in his, the Italian led her down the hall and into his bedchamber where an elegant dress and necklace were on display, at the foot of his California king bed, begging to be worn. Jennifer left his hold as she stepped toward the items, reaching out to test the softness of the red satin. The material was sexy, smooth and beautiful. Jenn could see the 'Rasario' tag and had to hold in what she really felt, which was the desire to greedily scoop the dress into her arms and jump up and down on the bed in excitement. She refrained.

"Anthony, are these for me?"

"Yes, silly. Who else could they be for? Let me help you into them."

Jennifer held her arms up for him to lift her sweatshirt up and over her head, leaving her naked chest open to him, anxious for his touch. He swooped down and pressed his warm, plump lips to the spot where her jaw and neckline meet. She immediately opened herself to him, neck moving to the side, inviting him to nuzzle closer. He continued a trail of kisses, dragging his lips across her ivory skin, reaching their destination at her clavicle. His fingertips glided across her flesh, tugging her nipples and then swirling gently over her areole. His hands trailed further. His target was the waistband of her shorts. All it took was a hook of his thumb and a quick snap and they fell to her ankles.

Anthony turned away to retrieve the dress from the bed, bunching it up, making it easy for her to get her arms into. As her head and arms poked through, he let go, allowing the material to fall. He put his hands on her waist, tugging at the material, guiding its way over her curves.

"Turn around."

She did so and immediately felt his touch return to her hips. He pulled her into his chest and just held her for a few moments, before stepping back and moving her hair out of his way. He tortured her, moving the zipper ever so slowly, his warm breath tickling the back of her neck. With the zipper in place, he reached back to the foot of the bed. This time he retrieved the necklace. Gold encased stones, one green and two blue. It was beautiful and exotic.

"Hold your hair out of my way, please, darling."

She did as she was told. He lowered the cool metal to her décolleté and wrapped the strands around her neck. He quickly closed the clasp and Jenn dropped her hair. He spun her towards him, placing a soft kiss to her lips and squeezing her ass through the satin.

He picked her up and placed her at the foot of the bed. Turning towards his closet, he slid the doors wide open. He then retrieved a small white box and returned to Jenn, kneeling before her. He removed the lid to reveal strappy heels. They slipped right onto her feet as he secured them at her ankles. His hand slid up her leg as he pushed the skirt higher, gliding along her inner thigh. He moved up on his knees so his mouth could reach her center. He gave her one long stroke of his tongue and a sloppy wet kiss to her clit. It was just a tease, leaving her desperate for more. However, he quickly stood and grasped her hand.

"Let's go. I've already moved our reservation back once and we don't want to be late."

Chapter 7

From tiptoeing to walking and walking to sprinting, Jennifer Caman was falling in love with her Italian. She knew she shouldn't, but here she was. She had spent the entire drive allowing anxiety to keep her out of being present with Anthony. He made her feel like he could take care of her, but so many others had made her feel that way before and had still left. Would Anthony really handle the problem with Maybella? Did he understand the severity of the threat? She would be the one to receive the biggest impact, basically being shunned from the salon community. He would maybe get teased for a couple weeks and then everyone would forget about it. She just hoped he understood she was more than his play toy and she had her own things to do and to deal with outside of him.

Anthony pressed a kiss to her temple and tightened his hold around her waist. They hadn't buckled up and this way, he was able to get her as close to him as possible. She was practically sitting on his lap. The luxurious black seating felt cool beneath her thigh that was exposed from the slit in her dress.

"Where do you think we're headed, princess?" The question pulled her away from her thoughts and brought her back into the moment with him.

"Hmm, I have absolutely no clue. I'm sure I'm in for a real surprise though."

Anthony leaned into his headrest with a satisfied smile.

"Hey, how many pet names do you think you'll end up coming up with for me? I mean… Princess? Peach? What's next Princess Peach?"

Anthony chuckled. His left arm resting on the door and propped under his chiseled chin. "We'll just have to wait and see. Won't we?"

Jennifer smiled and leaned in to kiss him on the cheek. Who would've thought that just hours ago she had received her first ever spanking and it had been administered by this very man? It surely hadn't left Jenn's memory just yet, her behind still tender and warm to the touch.

She felt the car glide to a gentle stop as Gerard turned around. "All right, you two, we have arrived."

Jenn looked to Anthony, waiting to follow his lead. He returned her look with a smile and taking her hand in his, opened the car door. He stepped out and turned to help his lady to her feet. Once both were outside the car, Jennifer could see where they were. They were in San Francisco's upper echelon downtown area and to the right of them was a big and beautiful building. It looked more like a hotel than any restaurant Jenn had ever been to. She thought she recognized the place, probably from passing by it on her way from the salon to school. It had large glass windows, giving onlookers a full view of what lay inside. It had an art deco feel and looked like the sort of place the Eagles might've been singing about in the song, *"Hotel California"*. Jennifer felt the uncovered skin of her arms flash with goosebumps as she took it all in. Her feet glided beneath her. She felt outside of herself as Anthony held the door open for her, ushering her in. In her heart, she felt trepidation hidden within. She had no reason to be afraid.

Even though this was all new and she felt she should run, she found herself falling deeper and deeper into the restaurant atmosphere. People ate in separate, secluded rooms. Everything was private. There was a man leading them to their table. Further and further back they traveled. She knew she would be lost if she tried to find her own way out. She held tighter to Anthony's firm bicep, red nails digging in slightly. They were led into a dark room that smelled of Marlboro reds and Prada L'Homme. There was just one round table in the corner with a circular booth around the far side of it. The back of the booth reached three quarters up the wall and there was a chandelier hanging over the center of the smooth marble surface of the table. It appeared to be an exact replica of the chandelier that had been at the entrance of the restaurant.

The two went to opposite ends of the booth and slid to meet each other at the center. Anthony pressed eagerly into her thigh that brushed near his. His fingertips greedily kneading her skin. He faced her and as she looked deep into his eyes, there was darkness within them she hadn't seen before. His hold on her leg dug deeper as he leaned in. Jennifer believed he was coming in with a passionate kiss. Her mouth was open, ready, willing. She was met with shock. Instead of firm softness, she was met with sensual pain. She never thought she liked pain before, but that bite to her bottom lip had made her belly flop in a way gentleness would never have been able to do. The first bite was swiftly followed by a second, but this one was at the soft lobe of her ear. He moved his tongue across her jawline and up to the bitten lobe he had just left, stopping and swirling circles with the tip of his tongue, before his lips came down to gently suck at their target.

Jennifer gasped and instantly felt heat rushing to enflame the tips of her ears and cheeks. Just as she let out a soft moan from Anthony's touch, the young man who had led them to their booth returned with a dark and foggy wine bottle and two glasses. The bottle had a gold shield plastered across it. She couldn't help but jump a little when the man popped the cork from the bottle, fog escaping the top. As the man filled their glasses, Anthony's hand wandered further up the slit in her dress. His fingers found her soft, thick lips and stroked teasingly up and down each delicate fold. She was embarrassed to be touched in this way with their waiter still in their presence, but perhaps that was normal in a place like this.

The waiter left the room without a word. Do any of the employees here speak or are they trained to keep their mouths shut, she wondered? Anthony's piercing green eyes hadn't left hers since they had sat down, not to look at the waiter entering or even to take a wine glass into his other hand. His eyes peered at her over the glass as he took his first sip. It was intense and Jenn was scared to look away.

"Aren't you going to have some wine, dear?"

She nodded her head. In this place, it felt as if words weren't the usual communication. You were encouraged to speak in the language of bodies. She lifted the crystal to her lips, allowing the dark liquid to pass through and invade her taste buds. It was a heavy, musky flavor. She had never drunk wine like this, but she could get used to it. It was strong and intoxicating and she knew she should pace herself, but one sip quickly followed the next. Anthony watched her as she enjoyed the wine. She sensed his satisfaction growing with every tiny sip of hers. Soft rock played in the background, all instrumentals and no vocals. She relaxed into Anthony, head leaning on his shoulder as his fingers continued their game of going back and forth from teasing her lips and then plunging into her wet center. It was clear the goal wasn't orgasm here, but worship.

He was worshiping her, her body. The sensuality of the moment continued to build. It already smelled like sex in the little room though nothing had really happened... yet.

The waiter returned with a large white platter of dainty hors d' oeuvres and Anthony's warm touch retreated, leaving her cold and anxious for him and his return. He took one of the delicacies and lifted it to her lips, delivering the food to her mouth with the same fingers that had just been buried within her. She willingly opened, eager for the taste, her mouth watering. It was a roasted sweet potato slice topped with whipped feta cheese, pomegranates, and figs and a rich brown drizzle that tasted sweet. She hummed her approval and reached for her own bundled sphere, lifting it to Anthony's lips, returning the favor. Anthony pulled her legs up across his lap and the two continued feeding the other until there were just three bites left on the tray.

Anthony and Jennifer leaned into each other at the same moment. He had his hands on her waist, pulling her in. Her hands held his face within them and encouraged him into a deeper and more passionate kiss with her. She moved her arms, wrapping them around the back of his neck and his grip on her waist pulled her into a hug. Their lips danced together: strong, steady, and hungry. He found her bottom lip completely within his own and didn't let go, harshly sucking and biting. She moaned into the kiss, desperate for every ounce of him she'd be permitted to have. At this point, she couldn't care less who saw, whether it was the wine or her feelings for him or a combination of the two, she wanted him.

When the two finally broke apart, out of breath and heated, they were surprised to find dinner had already been served. Before them sat plates of filet mignon, roasted asparagus, and garlic mashed potatoes. It was drizzled in a thick, red wine, pan sauce. They immediately unrolled the fine linen napkins that were wrapped around the shining silverware. As they cut into their steaks, the music over the speakers switched to something much harder and louder. Heavy guitar and drums blared. There was a refrain in the instruments and a woman's sensual voice filled the room, washing over them. The words "you are beautiful and sick like me" were heard clearly before the guitar riff cut back in.

As Jennifer took her second bite, a new man walked backwards into the room, before turning around. He had thick, black cuffs around his wrists and a hard-plastic mask. There was no expression to the mask and the only other item of clothing he wore were tight, latex briefs. Coiled in his hand was the handle of a dog's leash and at the other end was a woman, she was on her hands and knees, crawling after him. At the end of the leash, wrapped around her throat, she wore a dog's collar that was covered in sharp, metal spikes. The way she crawled was all hips and scapula. Her hips held her as she kept eyes locked on the man with the mask. Her breasts were held up by a leather corset and complimented by a matching thong, buried deep within her plump ass cheeks. Once the duo reached the center of the room, they stopped, and the woman began dancing sensually across the floor. Her body moved fluidly as she thrust her hips repeatedly towards the floor. Her body glided as she kept pace with the music. The man undid the leash and threw it across the room, metal clanking as the clasp hit the wall. He pulled her to her feet as she wrapped a leg around him. The leg that hooked around the man's waist stabilized his pet as he dragged her across the floor and then flipped her around to give her a classic dip as if they were simply performing your everyday waltz.

The room become steamy as a fog machine pumped out thick clouds. The fog machine was positioned above the booth and pointed downward. Jennifer was amazed to find she could smell the latex that constricted the male performer. She hadn't had another bite of her dinner and had to make sure her mouth wasn't hanging open. Anthony barely reacted, possibly well accustomed to the restaurant's style of entertainment.

The masked man lowered his woman to the ground where she immediately returned to the sensual position she had been in before. Jenn's heartrate skyrocketed as she realized the woman was now making her way toward them beneath the table. Jennifer was under the impression the minx would make an attempt to seduce Anthony. However, she quickly realized who her real target was. The laser focus the woman had held for her master was now directed at Jennifer who watched as she approached. She grasped Jenn's ankle and tugged. It was enough to shock her, but gentle enough to not hurt her or have her flying from the bench. She was now at the edge of her seat. She couldn't look away as the female entertainer trailed a line with her tongue from her ankle to the inside of her knee. The woman's tongue was warm and wet, leaving the skin that had already been licked, cool.

This was when Jennifer saw the whip, which was now in the man's right hand. While she had been distracted, he must've turned and grabbed the torture device from the rack behind him, which Jenn only just now noticed. It was full of different size whips of various colors and materials. He grabbed his partner and yanked her out from beneath the table, now lying flat on the ground with her back accessible to the masked man. Her face was covered by her hair, which was sprawled out around her. The man meticulously whipped her over and over, her screams and his blows clearly timed to be in rhythm with the song which now played. He didn't ease up on her until her back was covered in welts at which point she stood up and went to sit beneath the doorway on her knees, facing away from the onlookers, her hands resting on her lap with her palms facing up.

At this point, Anthony leaned in, hot breath flooding the side of Jennifer's neck. "That's how I plan to position you later." His voice was raspy and was more of a growl than a whisper.

The masked man turned to face Jenn. She could see his dark eyes from the holes in his mask and they were fixated on her own hazel orbs. She held her breath as he reached his hand to her, arm outstretched. Was she really supposed to go with him? She looked to Anthony for answers.

"Go ahead, darling." With his instruction, he gave her a little shove with his body, directing her out of the booth. She slid out from her seat and nearly tripped as she stepped towards the intimidating man. She gently lifted her small hand and placed it in his much larger one. He guided her closer to the center of the room where he and his pet had enacted their scene. He took the hand he still held and bent it to rest in the small of her back, moving her toward her dinner table, showing her she was expected to bend over the table with her bottom in the air. She was nervous, but excited as she folded herself for the masked sadist. She was pleased to find she could still keep eye contact with Anthony. A sly smile played at the corner of his mouth as he watched her be so obedient. The masked man raised one strong arm with whip in hand, smacking it across the red satin that covered Jennifer's behind. She gasped, but it wasn't as painful as she expected. She could feel warmth pooling between her feminine folds. She hoped Anthony would take her home after this. With each snap of the whip, the desire within Anthony's eyes grew. After three spanks, the masked man and his collared woman left, leaving Anthony and Jennifer alone to finish their dinner.

Anthony turned to face her as she finished off her last bite of potato. "Well, what do you think?" It could've been the wine, or the performance, or even just the way he was looking at her, but she was ready to pounce. She had never wanted anyone so badly and she could only hope dessert would be fast or that they would skip it, altogether. The wine had her buzzed enough she wasn't overthinking or judging herself for being into such a strange and scary show.

When she heard herself speak, she didn't recognize the voice. She felt like a more grown up version of herself, the version she knew just needed to be unlocked. She could take what she wants. She didn't have to feel so ashamed.

"Why don't you touch me and find out?" She taunted him by slowly running her hands up both his thighs as she was seated at an angle, completely facing him. She knew she could get in big trouble with him for her sass, but she didn't care. There was a part of her that wanted to see how much she could provoke him.

At once, his hands snapped into her hair and yanked her head into position below him and against his chest. His hold was relentless. He was clearly not in the mood for teasing and would use his power to bring her back under control if she tried to push his buttons.

"Watch your tone, little missy." He bit the side of her cheek beneath her ear before quickly scraping her ear lobe with his teeth as well. "Don't forget there's a wall of whips over there and I could easily have you back over this table in seconds."

She tried to pull away as the waiter entered with their dessert, but Anthony held her in place, crashing his lips down on hers. It was like he wanted the waiter to see, if only to prove she belonged to him. She tried to resist him, but soon melted into the kiss. That was all Anthony had needed as he then allowed her to sit up straight to assess the dessert that had been delivered for them.

"Airy Ghana chocolate cake & mousse au chocolate with coconut ice cream," Anthony declared as if he was reading a mail order dessert catalog listing.

"How do you know?"

"You put your order in with the chef when you make your

reservation, and this just so happens to be my favorite." Then, as if letting her in on a secret, he leaned in and added, "It tastes almost as sweet as you."

Jennifer blushed. Oddly enough it was one of the best compliments she had ever received. The dessert was rich and satisfying. The cake moist, the mousse smooth, and the coldness of the ice cream paired well with the warmth of the cake. She finished hers before Anthony and with a sneaky swoop of her index finger, she stole a bite of his mousse. He opened his mouth to object, but Jenn made a point to lick the fluff from her finger sensually, showing off the length of her tongue before closing down on her finger and sucking. She then, slowly, withdrew her finger from her pink lips, holding eye contact with Anthony the whole time. She wanted to be sure he watched the entire thing.

He shook his head before asking, "What am I going to do with you?"

"Take me home and tie me to your bed?" Her eyes were full of hope, doing the begging her pride wouldn't allow her to do openly with words.

"You know I would love nothing more, but the evening's not over yet. I have one more surprise in store for you."

Jennifer bit her lower lip. It was sweet he wanted to do all this for her, but she didn't know if she could make it. She was already so turned on and desperate for him. It felt like the entire evening, up until this point, had just been teasing and she was ready for the real deal. She didn't want to be teased any longer. She wanted him.

"I don't know if I can make it any longer... I want you." She felt embarrassed. She didn't like having to be the one to ask for it, but here she was. She couldn't help herself.

"You won't have to wait much longer. Just listen and follow me." He took her hand and they slid out of the booth together.

Anthony guided her out of the room they had been dining in, and led her down a corridor to the left as opposed to returning the way they had come in. The corridor was dark, only being lit up by real antique sconces that held white taper candles. There were no doorways for several feet and Jennifer couldn't see the end of the hallway for a few minutes. Her hand, still engulfed in Anthony's larger one, grew warm and sticky, a physical sign of her inward trepidation. After walking for what felt like much longer than it really was, the floor began to thump beneath their feet. Jenn secretly hoped it was from music and the building didn't have a life of its own.

After walking a bit further and feeling the beat of the music beneath them growing stronger, Jenn saw a single door. It was black and didn't look glamorous like the rest of the building had. Anthony reached out for the black handle, twisting and thrusting the door wide open to reveal a stairwell. He also released the music, which was so loud, it practically hit them in the face. As they walked down the concrete steps, Jenn trailing behind Anthony, she felt the beats pulsating on the hand railing. She felt like she was walking into her own funeral. It no longer felt like a decadent space, but like a cellar. She didn't know if she could make it to the bottom of the steps because everything within her screamed to turn around and run, but her curiosity drove her forward.

Reaching the bottom, her claustrophobia was set free. Turning right they were no longer encased within the stairwell but standing at the entrance of what appeared to be a club. There was a large man in a tuxedo standing guard at the entrance with a closet for coats off to the side and a red bar separating them from the party inside. Just as Anthony gave his name to the bouncer a woman's scream pierced through the music. Jennifer suddenly realized this might not be the typical nightclub she was used to and, instantly, her nerves stepped back in.

"It's Friday, Mr. Giuliani. You know the drill."

Receiving the message, Anthony began removing his suit jacket and unbuttoning the cuffs at his wrists. He then hung the coat in the closet beside them.

"The lady too."

Anthony rested his palm in the small of her back and guided her to the corner of the little entryway. He leaned into her and just barely whispered, "You have to remove an article of clothing to gain access."

She immediately bent over to undo the clasps on her heels when the brute of a man grunted out, "Shoes and jewelry don't count. The rule is an article of *clothing*."

Her heart trembled. All she had on was the dress and she hadn't worn a bra or underwear beneath. She looked to Anthony with desperation in her eyes, hoping he would understand the dilemma and not find her annoying for not wanting to be naked in front of a bunch of strangers. She was sure he had probably interacted with many much more confident women than she. Maybe if she had been here before it'd be different, but this was her first time and she had absolutely never been in a place like this before.

Anthony stepped away from her side, making an attempt to level with the bouncer. He lowered his voice to the point Jenn couldn't hear what the two were saying and it made her feel very self-conscious.

She sensed the two had come to a resolution when the bouncer's mouth relaxed into a smirk, not seeming quite so serious anymore.

"If the lady doesn't want to follow the rules, she must receive a spanking from a dungeon master. She can wait with me while you go in and find someone willing, Mr. Giuliani."

Anthony drew near to her and gave her a side hug while pressing his lips to her temple. "I will be right back, darling."

Here she was, alone with a bouncer outside of some sort

of sex club, twiddling her thumbs and playing with the smooth material of her dress while she waited for her man to bring a dungeon master to spank her. What was a dungeon master? Was he a professional at giving spankings or something? Should she be more scared? Would it hurt more than Anthony's had? The bouncer and Jenn sized each other up awkwardly. It was hard to tell which one was more uncomfortable.

Finally, Anthony returned with a muscular man with a shaved head. He wore all black: dress pants, short sleeved button up, shoes, and a belt. He crossed his beefy arms in front of him, making himself look even more intimidating.

"So you're the little lady who has a problem with our rules? We're going to need to fix that. Our safe word for the evening for the entire club is 'velvet'. Follow me."

Jennifer glanced from the dungeon master to the bouncer to Anthony, looking for any sort of reassurance, which was finally received from Anthony as he held his hand on her waist to walk with her as they followed the dungeon master to her doom.

Taking in her surroundings, Jenn noticed the club looked nothing like she had assumed it would. She was expecting lots of black and stone, but instead she found the space had a very similar vibe to the restaurant upstairs. It was Hollywood glamour and the 1920s with naked men and women: some fucking, some punishing, some playing, but most watching. It looked as if the space had been designed specifically for kink. Everything was organized into different spaces for different fetishes and different purposes. The dungeon master was clearly leading them to the spanking area. There was an entire wall with back to back spanking devices and toys. Everything you could imagine. It was quite overwhelming to try to take everything in. Just one corner of the club could provide hours and hours of play.

The dungeon master had led them to an old wooden bondage stock that was on a circular platform. Jennifer was surprised to realize how excited she was.

"Anthony, you can have a seat."

In front of the spanking space, there were a few rows of seating, three leather benches to accommodate any voyeurs of which Anthony now found himself to be one.

The stock was already open, waiting for Jenn's delicate throat and wrists. After Anthony had sat down, the dungeon master nodded his head toward the device, encouraging her to step onto the platform. She did so and was followed by her punisher who stood beside the stock, ready to close it and put the locks in place.

"I think you can guess what I'd like you to do now."

She could guess and so she did. Her wrists shook as she laid them into their circular cut outs before resting her neck into the largest cut out. The master gently pushed the top half of the stock, letting it fall into its place with a thud, making Jenn flinch. He then walked to the other side of the stock securing the metal locks, which Jenn nervously listened to, as he snapped them into place.

The dungeon master walked away, leaving her up on the platform by herself, unable to look at Anthony. In fact, she was staring at the far wall that was covered in paddles, whips and belts. She felt anxious waiting for his return and hoped to God that only Anthony sat on the benches before her.

Just then, Jenn heard the music cut out and the dungeon master's harsh voice boomed over the sound system.

"Our little miss here didn't want to follow the rules, and now, we think she deserves to be spanked."

The music was now completely turned off and Jenn felt herself being spun on the platform. She was spun really fast for a loop and then stopped as she now faced those ominous leather benches. They were filling up with leather and lace and latex clad men and women. She could only hope they were far enough away they couldn't see how red her face was. Was it okay to look at the ground the entire time?

She felt the satin of her gown being lifted. She was appalled. She had thought she would be receiving the spanking over her clothes. Rough hands stroked up her pussy and then left her with a smack.

The master's voice was so low only she could hear him. "I see you're wet already, you naughty little girl."

She was turned back to the side. She could now choose whether to look at the wall of spanking implements or at the onlookers, but she wished she could see the dungeon master to get some idea of when he'd begin.

Again, his voice came over the speaker. "I need a volunteer to go pick me out something to spank her with." She swiveled her head to the left, curious to see who would raise their hands. Many hands shot up, but not the most important one. Anthony sat cool, calm, and collected.

A petite woman must've been selected because Jenn watched her bop her dainty way to the wall. She held her hand out, hovering over all of her options as if feeling their auras before choosing. She landed on a black one. It was long and thin with a sturdy handle. At the end appeared to be a small, rectangular rubber piece. It honestly reminded her of one of the little plastic spatulas Katie had at the apartment.

"Ah, yes! The riding crop…" The speakers belted out. Jenn watched the woman hustle to the dungeon master, disappearing from Jenn's line of sight before reaching him.

Suddenly, he appeared before her and crouched to get in her line of sight. He had no microphone, but the riding crop was in hand.

"Have you ever been spanked with a riding crop before?"

Jenn shook her head no.

"Have you ever been spanked before?"

Her voice came out small, childlike. "Once."

A big smile spread across the dungeon master's face before leaving her sight once again.

He apparently had walked back to his microphone.

"We have a newbie here everyone! This will only be her second spanking. Ever."

Whoops and hollers spread throughout the club. Her observers clapped and cheered for her which surprisingly relaxed her, made her feel more comfortable, and even squeezed a smile out of her.

Her behind grew cold waiting for her 'punishment'. From behind her, she heard the man's voice again. This time without the microphone and without being projected throughout the entire room.

"Nice work, Anthony."

What did he mean by that? Then, it dawned on her. She must have some marks from her earlier spanking at the hand of her Italian.

Swat! Her first smack from the riding crop was delivered. It was nowhere near as hard as Anthony's had been and it made contact with the roundest part of her behind which had the most cushioning. However, the sound of it was deceiving, ringing out for the crowd to hear. It made her flinch in shock before making her pussy ooze with dampness. She loved being watched and she knew how hot this probably looked.

"Let us hear you scream!" The request was followed by a chorus of 'yeahs' and approvals before being reprimanded by Anthony's familiar voice.

"You better watch yourself, Johnny." Did he know every single person in the building?

"How many swats do we think she needs?" the dungeon master cried out.

A lot of voices with numbers called out, but the one that rang out above the rest was the number ten.

Another delicious snap was delivered to her ass. This one hurting a bit more as it landed in the crevice between her butt and thigh and must've been over one of her marks from Anthony. She gave in to the crowd and the desires of her audience. She screamed, loud. It wasn't even exaggerated. It was completely to scale with the force the dungeon master used.

Smack after smack after smack met her pale cheeks, reddening them more and more with each hit. The fiery warmth rising with each second. Her face was almost as warm as her ass from excitement, from embarrassment, and from adrenaline. The room counted with the dungeon master after each spank, "seven, eight, nine…"

The last wallop was the heaviest and most painful of them all. He had paused between nine and ten so she hadn't been as prepared. She bit down on her bottom lip from the strength of it.

"Ladies and gents, give it up for our new friend."

The room exploded. Jenn couldn't believe she had made it through something so far out of her comfort zone and she could practically feel her confidence skyrocketing.

The dungeon master lowered the bottom of her dress, slipping it over her pink, sore flesh. He then undid the locks and raised the top portion of the stock, freeing her from her bondage. He helped her find her footing as she stood up and placed both hands on her shoulders. He had a look of pride in his eyes and what had been previously unreadable was now all warmth. He seemed like a giant teddy bear.

"Enjoy your night. You've earned it."

Chapter 8

Jennifer was experiencing the most mundane of Mondays. She had had such a brilliant weekend with Anthony that she never wanted to have to return to work or school.

She now sat in the corner of the salon with a mannequin, working to perfect her blowout. She was happy for the bit of solitude the project provided as she wanted to avoid Maybella at all costs, who was also doing her best not to interact with her. Anthony had said he would fix the problems with the antagonist, but if this was what things were like 'fixed', she wasn't any more at ease. Maybella hadn't openly threatened Jenn again, but her eyes said it all. If Jenn had any questions, she wouldn't receive any answers. She just got the most earth-shattering glare and then instructions to, in nicer terms, get the fuck out of her face. The message was quite clear. Maybella would not be doing anything to mentor Jennifer in any way, shape, or form. The young stylist would just have to deal with it because she couldn't confront Monica about the issue out of fear that Maybella would stick to her aforementioned promises. Her fate was decided: every Monday from here on out would be busy work and dicking around and staying clear of Maybella.

To be honest, Jennifer didn't think she needed much help with blowouts. She already felt fairly confident in them and felt she was wasting her time doing and redoing blowouts on a mannequin. She was just reaching the section she had clipped up at the crown portion of the head when she felt someone tap her on her shoulder, making her jump. She turned around with the blow dryer still kicking to find Monica with an anxious look on her face. She was definitely not her usual uppity self. Jenn immediately kicked the blow dryer off, stopping the obnoxious whirring.

"Mr. Giuliani wants us to have a meeting with him in the office. It seems like it's about something pretty serious."

The two girls made their way to the office that was at the far side of the salon floor and down a hall. Jennifer had no clue what the meeting could be about. Anthony hadn't mentioned anything to her and she had just been with him this morning. All the stylists cast curious glances, which didn't go unnoticed by Jenn. News spread like a wildfire in a salon like this and anything that ever happened would be discussed extensively by every employee.

Opening the office door, Jennifer and Monica found Anthony Giuliani had already made it to the room and was seated behind the desk. An extra seat had been dragged into the small space and Maybella was seated on the other side of the desk, closest to the doorway.

"Ms. Caman and Ms. Monica, please take a seat."

The women exchanged nervous looks and did as they were told. At least Jenn now had some idea of what this could be about as Maybella was already here. Hopefully, whatever was about to happen would make things better and not worse.

Jennifer sat to the far-left in the extra seat that had just been added to the arrangement a few minutes before. The metal chair was cold and stiff and didn't serve to make Jenn feel any more comfortable. The rigid back of the seat leaned too far back. If she sat in the chair the way it was meant to, she would look like she was slouching. So, she leaned forward. Her ankles were tightly crossed to keep herself from nervously bouncing and her hands were pressed to the seat beneath her thighs to keep herself from biting her nails or picking at her cuticles. Most importantly, she absolutely refused to look at Maybella and she kept trying to lock eyes with Anthony to give herself some sort of assurance that everything was okay, but she received nothing. She actually felt like she had no private or personal relationship with Anthony in this moment. It was like she really was just some student who was assisting and being helped out by the Giulianis. She didn't like it.

Anthony sat tall and strong, filling up the small space with his masculine presence. His jaw was clenched, making him appear much more intimidating and uptight than he really was. His expression was completely unreadable and not one of the three girls could anticipate what he would say next. In front of him, on the desk sat a bundle of forms, but it was too hard to tell what they said as they were upside down and far away.

"As you all know, Ms. Caman is a part of our prodigy program or at least, I believe you all know. Maybella, if you were unaware previously, now you know."

Jenn took this moment to glance at Maybella finally, but there were no signs she was at all shocked by this revelation.

"I would like to start off by saying I owe you ladies absolutely nothing. I don't have to explain myself. I could say you're all fired and that'd be it."

He paused, clearly wanting the girls to soak up the magnitude of what he had said and understand his power over them.

"However…" Thank goodness he spoke again. Jenn was

beginning to believe he was about to fire them all. "I want to give you the opportunity to ask questions, understand where I'm coming from, and to make this right."

"What's the problem, Anthony? I have stuff I need to get done before my client comes in."

Jennifer couldn't believe her ears. Maybella's tone was dripping in disrespect and did she really call him by his first name? She had never heard any employee refer to him as 'Anthony', ever.

"I'm getting to that. You should know to watch your tone with me, Maybella, and I've reminded you many times, you're to refer to me as Mr. Giuliani. My first name is off limits to you."

Anthony looked like he was furious. Jenn had yet to see this intensity from him. Even when he had been upset by her manners with Gerard, he wasn't ever this stern with her.

"Ms. Caman, this will be news to you, and only to you, as the others are already aware. Years ago, when Maybella first started working at Giuliani's, she and I were intimate. The relationship we had was strictly sexual and never romantic. How I went about that relationship is something I am not proud of and since then, I have refused to fraternize with employees. I was greatly in the wrong back then and there was a lawsuit. That being said, I bring this up to assure you that any sort of animosity you feel from Maybella has nothing to do with your styling skills or professionalism, but rather because of a grudge she holds from our prior relationship."

Anthony paused, clearly allowing Jenn some time to process what he had said. Why hadn't he said anything sooner? If there was a lawsuit over their relationship, could there be a legal aspect of Jenn's relationship with him that she was unaware of which could get in the way of her career? She felt she should make some sort of response, to at least acknowledge she had heard him, but nothing came out. She was unsure of the emotions she was feeling: jealousy, anger, hesitancy, fear? He seemed so upset. Was he going to end whatever it was they had together?

She looked at Anthony and finally some sort of familiarity glimmered in his eyes. He no longer seemed angry, but sad. Was he disappointed in himself? Did he care what she thought or was he just hoping he wasn't in the dog house?

He turned to the other two women.

"Now, Maybella and Monica, Jennifer and I do have a connection. We have been intimate and we are moving forward. I intend to make her my girlfriend."

Maybella scoffed, but Monica reached out and squeezed Jenn's hands, which were now sitting on her lap. In this moment, Jenn couldn't be more thankful for Monica and for the instantaneous friendship they had. It was comforting to know she didn't judge Jenn. That was so important to her. She hated the thought of anyone not liking her or disapproving of her.

"Maybella, I am aware of the threats you have made to Jennifer in regard to her career. Jenn, I'd like you to tell Monica what you told me."

Tears welled behind Jenn's eyes. She knew in this moment, Maybella was the one who should feel stupid, but somehow she was the one who felt like the biggest idiot. Biting into her bottom lip, she reflected on how silly she must seem. Sleeping with someone so far above her and then having him save her and take care of her every problem and worry. Was she a baby?

Monica squeezed her hand again, breaking her out of her thoughts, but also breaking away the tear that had built up and had been waiting along her lower eyelid. Jenn quickly brushed it away, mortified. Looking into Monica's eyes, Jenn felt her mouth go dry. As much as she hated Maybella, getting her into trouble wasn't going to feel good.

"Whenever you're ready." Anthony's voice had returned to his usual caring and considerate tone he always used with her. He no longer sounded like the haughty businessman, but as the man she was growing to love. This motivated her to speak the truth.

"On my first day, right after you introduced me to her, Maybella hugged me and as she was hugging me, she whispered into my ear that she knew about Anthony and me. She said I'd better not make her upset or she'd ruin me."

Monica's eyes flooded with sympathy as her hand moved from Jenn's, flying to her mouth, clearly displaying her shock. Monica wasn't permitted the chance to respond, Maybella's high-pitched and whiny voice broke through. She was ready to attack.

"Oh, please. If you honestly, believe I would say all that, you're out of your mind. There's nothing wrong with a bit of friendly teasing for the newbie. Ever heard of hazing? What I said was nothing."

"That's enough, Maybella," Anthony bit back at her. There was no hint of letting up or being cordial with the bitch.

"Now that we all have been made aware of what this meeting is about, let's move on. Action has been taken. I have spoken with my lawyers and with our HR department in regard to this matter. As Jennifer and I began seeing each other before she was awarded prodigy by my *mother*, who had no prior knowledge of Ms. Caman and my relationship, our relationship is completely legal and separate from her position at Giuliani's. Maybella, there is nothing you can use legally against me or Ms. Caman to threaten her reputation within the beauty community."

Pfft. Did Maybella really just *pfft* Anthony? She had absolutely no right to do that, but then again Jenn hadn't heard much after hearing they weren't in the wrong. She was exhausted from the stress of the entire interaction and wanted to leave the office, go home, crawl into bed and cry out in relief.

"Then, I guess you won't mind if I discuss this with my lawyers also?" Maybella's retort oozed with malice and a viciousness Jenn had never seen in another person in her lifetime.

"You confer with your lawyers all you want. I have documentation organized here for you to look through. I also had one put together for Monica." He tossed a packet to each one of the women.

"I didn't think you'd need one, my dear, but I can also make you one, too, or we can talk about it more later." With this statement, Anthony's full attention was on Jenn and it was definitely the sort of attention only girlfriends receive. Would he make it more official soon? Was Jenn ready to be that public with him?

"Finally, seeing as your threat was defamation across all Giuliani locations as well as bullying, which are not supported in the Giuliani's code of conduct, we do have grounds to fire you."

"Are you joking? There is absolutely no way you can fire me." Maybella's voice raised in tone and in infuriation with each word, making both Monica and Jenn cringe and Anthony fume before cutting back in and continuing with what he had to say.

"However... I am not a monster and do not wish to fire you. Do not give me reasons to feel otherwise. I have decided to have you relocate to another Giuliani's location and if we hear you're discussing Jenn and my relationship with coworkers or anyone else for that matter, we will reconsider letting you go."

Maybella continued on, speaking over Anthony as if he

wasn't making any sort of communication at all. "You can't do that! All of my clients are local to this area and—"

"*Enough.*" Anthony didn't yell, but he definitely commanded the room and had enough force behind this one word to make any sane person cower.

"Erm… Mr. Giuliani? What would you like us to do with Jenn on Mondays now that she won't be able to train with Maybella?" Monica sheepishly asked.

With this question, Anthony plastered a wide smile across his face, obviously ready for the prior conversation to be over.

"Well, that is up to the two of you and what you believe is best and makes the most sense." Anthony got up from his seat and rounded the desk. Now, very near to Jenn, as if conspiring with her, he said, "Let's get dinner late tonight once you get out of school, darling."

He held her arm gently and gave her a quick kiss before exiting the room.

Jennifer lazily slung her purse over her shoulder and bent over to pull up the handle on her rolling hair case. She left her phone and case at her station, running to fill up her water bottle in the break room before she left. She was going directly home from school where she assumed Anthony would be waiting for her so they could have dinner together. She was absolutely starving and would be happy with anything he had planned, even if it was them popping a frozen pizza in the oven and cuddling up on the couch for a movie. She was exhausted from all of the Maybella drama and just wanted to relax, but would still be okay if Anthony wanted to go out. She just wanted to see him and to have him hold her. She felt she should be a little upset with him for not telling her earlier about his history with Maybella, but she wasn't. She was going to talk about it with him and move on.

Water bottle in hand, purse on her arm and ready to leave, she returned to her station where her phone sat, face up. The screen was lit up and a text message was displayed across the lock screen.

From Anthony: *Can't do dinner tonight. Business meeting went late. xoxo*

Her heart fell. She knew it wasn't the end of the world, but this was the first time he had ever had to cancel on her and it didn't feel good. She knew she had just had time with him this morning, but she needed to talk to him. This was no reason to get upset. Anthony is a busy man and this would probably happen again many times. Besides, didn't she just want to lay in bed and watch TV anyways? She could do that on her own and she would see Anthony tomorrow or the next day.

As she left the school and made her way to her car, she realized she was still starving and would need to figure out dinner for herself. There was no way in hell she was going to cook a real meal tonight so her only other option was takeout. She didn't want to sit down to eat somewhere by herself. Not tonight anyways.

She decided on sushi, veering into her favorite place's parking lot, which was conveniently an easy stop on her way home. Sure, they closed in thirty minutes, but they might be willing to make one more order. If not, she was sure a generous tip might persuade them.

Passing through the front door as the bell dinged her arrival, Jenn stepped to the front counter where a young, Asian man sat at a cash register.

"Hi! I'd like to make an order for takeout!"

"Sure, what would you like?"

"Could I just get one of your House Zen Platters?"

The cashier smiled with his entire face and nodded, typing her order into the computer.

"Forty-two dollars, please"

Jennifer pulled her phone from her back pocket and noticed another text that she would read once she had completed her order. She pulled her debit card from the wallet case that was attached to her phone. Swiping her card on the scanner, she waited for the man to hand her the receipt so she could sign. He furrowed his brows in confusion before aggressively tapping his computer a few times. A few seconds later, a *bleep* blared from the machine.

"I'm sorry, Miss. It says your card is declined."

Jennifer almost laughed at the mistake. There was no way that was possible.

"Run it again."

He rapidly started typing and pushing buttons before dejectedly looking at her and shaking his head.

Confused, she reached for her wallet and pulled out the credit card she used for gas and gas alone. She assumed the issue was probably a computer malfunction or her card needed to be replaced.

The credit card went through and Jenn was handed the awaited receipt and pen. She added her usual twenty-five percent tip and signed across the dotted line at the bottom. She graciously accepted her customer copy, folded it, and put it into her wallet.

She sat down on the bench by the entrance to wait for her order to be made. She took the time to read the text she had ignored.

Unknown Number: *"Check this out"* <*photo attached*>

Her reaction to the message was visceral. She had barely taken the image in before she leaped to her feet and ran to the bathroom, leaving the cashier greatly concerned. Luckily, the women's room was a single stall. She began stripping and laid on the floor, desperate for the coolness of the tiles. She had begun seeing splotches in her vision and she knew if she didn't cool herself off, she would've passed out. She didn't know how long she laid there. She didn't care if she died in that dirty bathroom. Just when she began to feel better, her mouth started watering and her tummy churned. She launched herself into a sitting position. Holding her hair back, she vomited. Even after she was finished, she couldn't stop dry heaving as tears streamed down her face.

Moments later, she forced herself to take deep breaths and slowly regained her composure. The heaving stopped and she was left with a hiccup and a bit of spit at the corner of her mouth. Sniffling and then blowing her nose in some toilet paper, she stood up. The mirror reflected a horrifying image: a woman recovering from a panic attack, eyes darkened from mascara and streaky foundation. She continued taking deep, measured breaths as she turned the right handle of the faucet. Icy water spurted out and she held her hands beneath the flow, welcoming the calming cold.

Brushing her hair over her shoulders, she left the small bathroom and reentered the world. She returned to her seat where she had received the upsetting text. The man had waited with worry etched into every inch of his youthful face.

"Are you okay, miss?"

Words felt like too much so she did the best she could while not making eye contact. She nodded. She knew looking at another human would break her back down and she couldn't afford another second of that. She wanted her food. She wanted her bed.

Jenn spent most of her drive home sobbing. At first, she tried to hold everything in, but she quickly realized there was no point. Unlocking the door to her apartment, Jenn stepped in to find Katie sitting on the couch. This was strange in and of itself because her roommate typically went to bed really early and was always in bed before Jenn got home on her late nights of school. Hopefully, she didn't notice how much Jenn had been crying. She definitely wasn't in the mood to talk about it.

Jenn offered a quick "hey" before crossing to the kitchen where she retrieved a diet coke from her organized shelf of the fridge. She then sat at their bar stool table in the dining room which was open to their small living room. She dug into her sushi, more and more realizing something weird was going on with Katie. The TV wasn't on and she didn't have her phone in her hands. She just sat by herself, arms crossed, and staring at Jenn as if she should know what was going through the girl's head.

In an attempt to break through the tension, Jenn offered her friend some of her sushi, even though she knew Katie hated the stuff. Her offer went completely ignored. Jenn had popped a large roll into her mouth, the sound of her swallowing amplified throughout the quiet space. It was awkward and uncomfortable.

"What the hell is going on with you, Jenn?"

So, Katie had noticed Jenn had been crying. How could she let her in without telling her the more private details she wished to keep to herself?

"It's just been a really long day and—" Jenn was cut off.

"I'm not finished talking, Jennifer. You've been so caught up in yourself. Everything is all about you. Since you've been spending time with Anthony, I've noticed a huge change in you. It's gotten to the point where you're a bitch all of the time. Being a bitch on a bad day is one thing, but it is all the fucking time now. You're rude and manipulative and constantly playing games with people. You act like you need to be babied and taken care of all the time and I'm sick of it. I'm done helping you with things. If you need something, ask your dick of a boyfriend."

What is this all about? Had Jenn been being a bitch? She hadn't thought she had. She actually felt like she was a really good friend. She always took the time to listen to Katie when she had complaints about work or about her own boyfriend. She hadn't asked her to do anything for her since she had driven Jenn to the bar weeks ago. Was this all because Anthony treated her so well while Lucas barely spent time with Katie? Could this all be because of jealousy or was there truth to what Katie said? What was this really about?

Jenn felt more tears coming on. Never in her life had she been attacked so verbally. It was punch after punch. How was she supposed to respond to all of that? Was there really any right response?

"I-I'm sorry to hear you feel that way. I honestly have no idea where any of this is coming from. I thought you and I were closer than this and I was completely unaware you had any problems with me."

"How could I not be mad at you, Jenn? I don't deserve to come home to notices on our door from the landlord, notices about you."

A notice? A notice of what? What could Jenn have done wrong that would warrant any sort of notice and if it was really about something Jenn did, why was Katie so worked up? She was capable of taking care of herself.

"Yeah, I come home to find a notice plastered to the front of our door. Apparently, last weekend the neighbors heard some screaming. They told the office it sounded like someone was getting beat up. They wanted to make sure no children lived with us because if there were, they were going to call Child Protective Services."

So they had heard Anthony giving Jenn her first spanking... how embarrassing. How was she supposed to explain that to Katie who was as vanilla as they come? Her boyfriend would only have sex with her like once a week and he definitely wasn't the spanking type. He actually seemed like a sub, not dominant at all. Then again, she shouldn't have to explain herself. It was nobody's business, but if they had gotten a notice about the noise, should she be worried? Should she be ashamed? She knew she wasn't into the most normal of things, but to have her oddities thrown in her face like this really hurt. She felt like a total freak.

"What the fuck has Anthony been doing to you? Is he abusive or are you two just big fucking weirdos? I know you're into some weird stuff, but that is not normal, Jenn. It's disgusting and disrespectful. Do you need to speak with a therapist? I have a number you can call if you need one."

Was she serious? She wasn't mentally deranged for wanting a good spanking once in a while. She had never felt so judged. Was there any truth to what she was saying? Jenn cared too much about what other people thought to not let this conversation get to her.

Should she respond?

"Katie, I can't do this tonight. I'm going to bed."

"You can do this tonight and you will. We need this sorted now."

With that comment, Jenn grabbed her purse and ran out the door. She was headed for her car and already had her keys in hand. Thank goodness she'd gotten her car back from the shop. Waiting for an Uber would've been the end of her.

Getting into her car, she went to Google maps and found the option for 'hotels near me'. She clicked the first one and began heading there just as Katie came running after her. The last thing she saw of the complex in her rearview mirror was Katie shaking her head with arms flung out in exasperation.

At the first stop light, she turned her location services off. She didn't want Katie following her. She also silenced messages from Katie as her phone was blowing up with message after message, long rants about how Jenn was messing up her life and chances at a successful future.

There were no more tears left for the rest of the night. Too much had happened in one day. If this had been a normal day that just so happened to have one negative blip of an argument with her roommate, she might still be crying. Now, she had nothing left.

Checking into the hotel lobby, Jennifer asked the concierge for a room for one for just one night. She handed him the card she had attempted to buy sushi with earlier. Once again, the debit was declined. The gentleman behind the desk suggested she relax in one of the comfortable chairs in the lobby for a few minutes and then check to make sure her accounts were in order. He must've seen the fury and the hurt within her eyes. It's probably all that could be seen. Under different circumstances, she knew he would've just told her that her card had been declined and then left her to fend for herself. She hated his pity.

She sunk into the plush embroidery of a Victorian style couch. Would it be all right if she just slept here? She was beyond exhaustion. Anywhere would do.

She unlocked her phone and swiped to find the Bank of America app. Using her fingerprint to gain access to her account information, she discovered that her account was, in fact, empty. This couldn't be right. Something must've been double charged, but it was too late to call the local branch or to stop by for assistance. She couldn't add the hotel to her credit card, racking up debt for items when she had nothing available to spend within her main account would make her anxiety far worse than it already was.

In defeated resignation, she made her way back out to her car. She climbed into her backseat, locked the doors, and made herself as cozy as possible. She needed to sleep and she was too tired to come up with any more plans. This was rock bottom. Why couldn't Anthony have cancelled on any other night? She knew if she called him and told him everything that had happened, he would rush to get her and come take care of her, but she couldn't allow that. Katie's words had gotten into her head, Maybella's words had pierced her heart, and the unknown texter's message had sucker punched her in the gut. She was too broken for Anthony to see her right now, all alone and curled up in the backseat of her Buick with hands beneath her head for a little pillow.

Before dozing off into a heavy nightmare-filled sleep, Jenn looked at the photo she had been sent. There, on her screen, was the most incriminating picture of herself she had ever laid eyes on. It was her, in the club and bound by the wood slats of the stock. Could Maybella be behind this and what were the sender's intentions for the photo?

Chapter 9

"You're going to have to find something to do on your own today, Jenn. I have nothing planned for us, but I did get it okayed for you to go get a new mannequin out of the closet to work on."

Since Jenn had been in the salon that morning, everything seemed unusual. People kept giving her funny looks and she hadn't received any perky greetings that were common for a bustling salon.

She was so thankful she had woken up early. She had been able to run home and get herself put together without Katie over her shoulder as she had already left for work by the time Jenn had gotten home from the hotel. Can you imagine the frostiness she'd receive from the other stylists if she had shown up late and not showered?

As Jenn walked towards the supply closet, she passed by the break room where she heard a few stylists speaking in hushed tones. Jenn wasn't the type to eavesdrop, but if stylists were speaking quietly, it must be about something important or serious. Standing against the wall to keep herself from being seen, Jenn leaned her ear towards the doorway just as her name was brought up.

"We all saw the three of them get called into the office. Maybella is gone now. I have no idea what was said, but I can't help feeling that she's not here because of something the new girl might've said. She seems sweet enough, but it's Maybella. I'm gonna side with my girl."

The other stylists responded in murmurs of agreement and understanding. Each one validating the other's feelings of malice toward the 'new girl', aka Jenn.

Jennifer couldn't believe what she was hearing. Sure, she understood why they were upset about Maybella being transferred, if they even knew she had been relocated. Maybe they thought she was fired, but why would they assume it was because of Jenn that she was gone? Had she told them about her and Anthony? I mean, what sort of power did she have as the new girl to remove another talented stylist? Why was she being seen as the culprit?

Not wanting to hear anymore and horrified by the possibility one of the girls could leave the room and discover Jenn listening in, she continued to her destination. Entering the supply room, she crossed over to the cabinet labeled 'mannequins'. She was just about to grab one when she turned around to the sound of heels on concrete. It was Monica.

"Jennifer, you know you can't just take one of those, right? Those are expensive. We're happy to have you use them, but our rule is you must pay half of their original price."

So she hadn't been approved to use one. Her Tuesday stylist was hoping to get her in trouble, further evidence everyone was out to get her since Maybella's departure. She knew she could tell Monica what had really happened, but Jenn didn't want Monica any more upset. Hearing Maybella's true nature yesterday really seemed to rock her. Besides, they couldn't relocate every single stylist who was mean to her.

Especially at this point, with the numbers growing by the minute.

"Oh, I'm sorry. I didn't know. My stylist doesn't have anything for me to do today. Would it be okay if I invited a model to come in for me to work on?"

"Yes, of course."

Jenn immediately pulled out her phone and began texting Lola. She was sure she would come in and the two of them could get food together before heading to school. Lola had been asking Jenn to give her a full head of highlights and this was the perfect opportunity to do so. Jenn was just making lemons into lemonade.

Making it back to her station, she began to prepare for her friend to get there. However, she wasn't so engaged in the task that she forgot what had just happened. The stylists surrounding her were out for blood. She felt she couldn't become too relaxed out of fear of what might be coming. After receiving that text, she knew someone was out to get her and had the means to do so. Would she end up telling Anthony? She hadn't wanted to burden him with anything else.

Lola arrived as gracefully as she did everything and Jenn began the lengthy process of foiling. She had had to ask for help locating all the supplies she would need from the closet, but now felt quite confident and was beginning to catch a flow as she applied fluffy, blue-toned lightener to each thin slice of hair before folding its foil casing. The two friends lost themselves in a discussion of hair and for just a moment, Jennifer wasn't thinking of her troubles: the photo, Maybella, Katie, or her empty bank account.

Jennifer worked both efficiently and consistently and found herself to be completing the last section of foils much sooner than she had thought possible. This now meant she could check some of those first foils she had placed to see how well they were lifting. Swiveling Lola in the salon chair, she lifted the back section she had started with and clipped some foils out of the way so she could get a better view. She unfolded that first foil down lengthwise before undoing the two thin folds on the outer edges and then finally opening the entire foil to reveal the hair beneath. What she saw was devastating to say the least. She wasn't quite sure what had happened, but what she had hoped would be a level 9 blonde was really a deep cobalt blue. This couldn't even be seen as a happy accident because although Lola was stunning, she was not the type of person who could pull off blue hair. What would Jennifer tell her poor friend?

Dumbfounded and stricken of all verbal communication, Jenn left from behind Lola's chair without another word. She attempted to appear cool, calm and collected, aware all eyes were currently on her. Where was she going? She wished she could say she was going out the front door and far far away, but she was really on the hunt for Monica. Hopefully, she would know what to do or would at least understand what might've created such a mess.

Jenn felt her phone buzz in her apron's pocket and quickly pulled it out. She found a text from Lola: *Where are you going? Is everything okay?*

Oh, God.

Finding Monica behind the receptionist's desk, she didn't get the chance to explain what was happening before Monica began bombarding her with questions.

"Honey, what's wrong? You look like you've seen a ghost. Is it Maybella? Did something happen with Anthony?"

Monica's questions flew from her mouth in a matter of seconds as she hopped up and grabbed Jennifer's hands, holding them out and inspecting her as if she were a little kid who had gotten into a biking accident.

Taking a second to take a deep breath and collect herself so as not to cry, Jenn tried to find the words.

"S-Something has-hasss happened. I'm not sure what, but I need you. It's Lola's hair."

Jenn must not have hidden how shaken she was very well because Monica immediately began to follow her back to her chair with an Army general level of seriousness. It was as if Jenn were in the middle of surgery and had called Monica in for her expert opinion.

When they arrived at the chair, Lola seemed quite worried as she was inspecting the foils. Did she have x-ray vision? There's no way she could see the hair through the aluminum coverings.

Jenn basically repeated the same thing she had told Monica to Lola with the addition of, "I am so sorry. We are going to figure this out." As she made a promise she had no way of keeping, she opened that first foil for Monica to inspect.

After swallowing as if in horror, Monica said but one command, "Take me to the supply closet and show me which lightener you chose."

In the supply closet, Jenn began to really lose her cool, which was signified by a tear finally escaping. She knew she felt terrible about this mistake, but also knew this feeling was amplified by the fact she hadn't gotten the best sleep spending the night in her car.

She pointed to the lightener she had been directed to use by another stylist whose name seemed to have slipped her mind. She realized then it might have been one of the girls she had caught talking about her in the break room. The lightener was in the corner of the top shelf. It was super far away from the other lighteners.

"Oh, Jenn... that's not a normal lightener. We just

received that. It's a new fashion color that lifts the hair 4+ levels and deposits pigment as it goes."

Why did it feel like she had been misguided on purpose? Sure, she should give her helper the benefit of the doubt, but after being sent that photo, she couldn't trust anyone.

"Jennifer, who told you to use that?"

The best they could do was slap a level 3 brownish black over top of every part of her hair and call it a day. The two friends had planned on getting lunch together, but after the blue lightener debacle, both decided against it. Lola hugged Jenn and attempted to assure her she wasn't mad at her. Even as she said it, there were tears pooled in her eyes, sure to spill over as soon as she got back to her car. She told Jenn she wouldn't be coming into school, even though she wasn't mad, she couldn't handle being at school today.

Jenn couldn't have lunch due to her empty bank account. Her best bet was to find the number Anthony had given her for his financial advisor and ask him if there was anything they could do. She was sure there had to be a mistake somewhere. There was no way she blew through that money so quickly. She rummaged through her car, throwing around her hair case, her makeup kit, and her duffle bag that held all of the items she would need for her state board test. She had to find the folder she had of all the papers from her first day at Giuliani's because she knew that was where she had to have put the number to the fee-douchie-whattie.

After much effort, she found the folder, hidden beneath her passenger side seat. Opening it, she perused the pages. She was looking for a sheet with a number sprawled across the top left corner.

She quickly grabbed the last paper and there it was: the

number for her money Yoda. Immediately, she began typing the number into her phone's dial pad. She waited as the connector rang five times before being picked up on the other line. An older man's gruff voice could now be heard.

"Yes?"

"Hi, sir. My name is Jennifer Caman." She explained who she was, what her situation was, and that it was urgent. She was then informed of what a fiduciary does and that looking through someone's bank accounts and making sure there were no errors was not a part of his job description. However, taking into consideration how desperate she sounded and her connection to Anthony Giuliani, he would meet with her in an hour at his downtown office. He also was sure to emphasize the fact he would only help her because of who Anthony is. Before hanging up, she gave him as much of her account information as she could while over the phone so he could start putting together a report. Here, she found out that he could access some of her information just by peeking into Anthony's files, but not a lot. For one thing, he could see exactly how much she made each paycheck and he could hear from her she was now completely drained of funds so you could say she was a little embarrassed and not very excited for their upcoming meeting. The man sounded stern and grumpy and not happy to be helping her out. What kind of hold did Anthony have over the people of San Francisco to be able to call in favors like this simply because of who he was? You'd think he was royalty or something.

After hanging up with the fiduciary, whom she was informed went by Mr. Robertington, Jenn sat in a McDonald's parking lot, in her car, watching Netflix and killing some time. She was just racking up reasons for Anthony to be disappointed in her... first blowing all the money she had and now she would be showing up late to school. Would he also be upset at her for wasting Mr. Robertington's time? He had been pretty upset with her for wasting Gerard's time. He had even given her a spanking for that offense. Would she be receiving another spanking and would she hate it like the last one or would she enjoy it like the whooping she'd received from the man at the club?

Upon arriving at the building that held Mr. Robertington's office, Jennifer discovered more anxiety than she originally thought she would experience over the meeting. Deep within her, she knew the truth. This was her doing and hers alone. Her fiduciary wasn't going to find any mistakes or doubled transactions. She had simply catered to her impulsivity. Not only had she bought herself any and everything she could have wanted, but she had spent so much on others and had given her money out like it was candy. She had come into such a fortune that it felt wrong not to share it. However, she did notice how comfortable her friends and family had gotten asking for 'help'... did her mom really need financing for a tummy tuck and did Steph really need new extensions? Jennifer knew she was in no position to decide as she had felt she *needed* red bottoms, which probably wasn't true. How would she explain all of this to Anthony and how would she find the money for food until her next pay day? She hadn't even bought groceries! She figured she didn't need to anymore since she could just eat out or order takeout... that probably hadn't been financially sound reasoning.

She didn't think she could do it. How could she go in and speak with a professional about this? Especially, after being told this wasn't even his job to do.

As she sat inside her car outside of Mr. Robertington's office, she saw Anthony and Gerard pull up in his shiny, black Bentley. Oh, no. She watched in trepid anticipation as Gerard opened the door, allowing Anthony to step out. Jennifer ducked her head, hoping it was just a coincidence he was here and he wouldn't notice her. She sat with her head under her hands, tucked down by the steering wheel, when she heard a gentle rapping on the driver's side window. Slowly, Jenn lifted her head to meet Anthony's unreadable gaze. She then rolled down her window.

"Get out, silly. Mr. Robertington called me and asked me to come and sit in on your meeting. Why are you hiding?"

"Am I going to be in trouble?" Jenn knew even as she said it, she was.

"Well, baby, that all depends on what Mr. Robertington has to say. Are you hoping to be in trouble?"

Shaking her head as she got out of the car, she tripped over Anthony, her nerves making her a hot mess. He steadied her by the waist and then slipped his hand lower to clasp her hand in his. Jenn thought she might be more terrified than when she was descending into that stairwell before.

The two of them made their way inside, leaving Gerard behind to wait for them. Entering the building, Jenn could tell this was an expensive and exclusive place to be having your finances managed. Innately, Jennifer knew she didn't belong. For a moment, she even questioned whether she belonged with Anthony. He was so far above her.

Anthony guided her to one of the closed doors that had a small metal plaque beside it that read, "Edward Robertington. Fiduciary." Anthony knocked on the taupe colored wooden door. Jenn noted the authority with which he knocked. It was no longer the gentle rap he had just blessed her car window with, but an assertive and steady knock. Anthony had stepped into his businessman mode. Jenn was beginning to realize he was only ever gentle or silly when he was with her and rarely was he like that with her if they were in the public eye.

Anthony's knock was met with a grunt, which was received

as an invitation to enter. They found themselves within a small office with a desk and a withered, old man behind it. His voice had sounded much younger over the phone or Jenn had just mistaken his gruffness for grumpiness as opposed to age, but maybe there was a little bit of both… the man had a keen likeness to Gandalf the wizard with a long white beard from Lord of the Rings. However, this wizard was wearing a suit.

"Jennifer Caman, meet my grandfather on my mother's side, Edward Robertington."

Edward chuckled as if he found Anthony's grandiosity amusing, which Jenn couldn't say she didn't also. It was kind of cute when Anthony got really formal. Teasing aside, it was impossible to hide her shock. She hadn't even met his parents yet and here she was meeting his grandpa. She wondered if he was upset to have such a meeting thrown on him so soon in their relationship.

Jenn reached across the desk to shake an unwilling hand. "It's a pleasure to meet you, sir." At this, Edward chuckled again. This time with more meanness behind it. "I wish I could say likewise."

Great, so the one member of his family she's had the opportunity to meet hates her. Amazing.

After receiving his hand back from Jennifer's pink polished and dainty hand, he began to lay copies of what looked like Jennifer's Bank of America account before both of them, one stack for Anthony and one stack for Jenn.

"Now, I must say I find it strange that you're paying your girlfriend directly from your account and such a large amount at that. Half of what you're receiving, Ms. Caman, would've been crazy enough. Your payments are absolutely ludicrous. Furthermore, the fact you've managed to spend Giuliani hard-earned money in just a few weeks nearly makes me sick."

"*Nonno*, I know Mom has already covered your opinions on this matter and has made it clear that, although we appreciate your input, we've made our decision on what we'd like Jennifer to receive and will discuss it no further. As for whatever you have to say about my relationship with Jenn or my involvement in her finances, you can either explain them cordially or not at all."

Jennifer wanted to turn into a pile of slime and ooze over the edges of her seat and onto the floor and through the vents. She had been nervous enough for this meeting without the added stress of meeting Anthony's family member and of said family member hating her guts. The tension in the room pressed in on her and made her chest feel heavy. Tears welled up in her eyes as Edward began to explain the sheets of paper he had placed before them. He rambled on, reading each transaction, disapproval dripping in his tone.

When he had come to the bottom of the list, dated a few days ago, when she had sent a PayPal amount to a girlfriend to get lunch after a breakup, he began to question her.

"What are all these cash transfers to various people that are in absurd amounts? Do you have some sort of drug problem? Are you buying drugs with this money? Why do you have so many people to pay off? What are you hiding?"

Overwhelmed and confused by the interrogation, Jenn sat dumbfounded, her mouth opening and closing in an attempt to form any sort of communication.

"Now, *Nonno*... I'm sure Jennifer has a logical explanation. Right, Jenn?"

He turned to face her, irritation in his eyes. Was he upset with her or with his *nonno*? He couldn't possibly believe what his *nonno* was saying, could he?

That's when it happened. The tears finally broke through as she explained how badly she knew she had managed her money and she was so sorry. Then, it seemed both men softened and they softened even more as she shared with them how much she had been spending on other people. She emphatically stated she had spent just as much, if not more, on herself and she understood the repercussions.

After her outburst, Edward asked her to go through her transactions and see if she could remember what the transfers to others were for and if she had given it as her own idea or if they had asked.

Together, she and Edward discovered she was spending more on others than herself and that it was only in the beginning they could be considered gifts. The rest were all given at her friends' and family's request.

———

Anthony had her give her keys to Gerard, while Gerard gave the keys to the Bentley to Anthony, who was now circling to the driver's side door. He clearly expected Jenn to follow after him. She hopped into the passenger seat and buckled herself in. She still couldn't get a read on her man. Was he upset over the financial meeting or was he just quietly collecting his thoughts?

As Jenn wondered about him. Anthony passed the road they needed to turn to take Jenn to school. What the hell was he doing?

"Anthony, where are we going?"

"Home." His voice was void of emotion. He could be pissed, apathetic, or ecstatic. Jenn had no clue and she was almost too frightened to question him. Almost.

"But what about school? I still need to go back to school. I can't go home yet."

He didn't respond but rather reached for his phone. He held it up to his face to do a voice command. "Call Ben Whitaker." He was beautiful in his assertiveness, jaw clenched and left fist curled around the steering wheel. His tan skin aggressively stretched over the features of his face. His beauty terrified, the intensity of his presence overwhelmed. It didn't matter how afraid she was of him when he got dark, her pussy still pooled for him insistently. "Hi, Ben. How are you? Jennifer Caman won't be at school today. Do not hold this against her. She should not have to make this day back up or be penalized for skipping."

Click. The call was over and Anthony made no effort to further communicate with Jenn for the rest of the ride home. Soft jazz played in the background, nothing that Anthony would ever choose to play on his own, but he didn't care enough to turn it off.

After they pulled up the drive and came to a full and complete stop, Anthony jolted the gear shift from drive to park. He slammed his door open and ran to Jenn's side so quickly she couldn't even think about getting out herself. He threw open her door and leaned across her to unbuckle her. Invading her space, she smelled his musky cologne. He picked her up, flinging her over his shoulder. He was bringing her inside and further– to his bedroom.

"Anthony!" But it was too late. She was in his room and bent over the bed. Her booty facing up, spanking ready as he ripped both her pants and underwear off. She had known it was coming, but now that it was here she was more scared than the first time. He had an unreadable air circling him and there was no way of reaching him. He was far away and unable to connect with her.

He left her, and because of the lowlighting of the room, and the position she was in, it was impossible for her eyes to follow where he was going. Her mind filled in the gaps. She could picture him inside that kink closet. What would he pick out for her?

She heard him coming back from the hallway. He was practically running. Without warning, he delivered the most gut wrenching swat to the back of her thigh. The sound of the smack made her jump and the pain had her shuddering. It felt like it peeled her skin. The sting was unbearable and nothing like anything she would have ever dreamt of or fantasized about. Her scream echoed throughout the loft and she wondered if Gerard could hear it from the garage. She actually turned to check if she was bleeding, it felt hot. She gasped at what she saw: Anthony had cut her, granted it was very small, but the imprint was bruising already and he was pulling his arm back to punish her further. Did he think her bleeding was nothing?

"Stop! I mean, *Apricots! Apricots!* For God's sake, Anthony, what the actual fuck?" Her shrieking had an amazing effect on her man. He snapped out of it and as he did, she watched his eyes change from a cloudy dark green to a clear sea foam color. He even shook his head as if he was confused by himself and what he was doing.

He was a Pitbull. He was dangerous for her and if he hadn't stopped, she would've run from him. She suddenly realized she loved him. Nothing mattered to her except her love for him. Anger issues could be handled and she found a new understanding of why she might need a safe word because without it, he might not have been able to stop himself. Unwelcomed tears skimmed from her cheek to the corner of her mouth and off of her jaw to the floor. Did he enjoy bringing her pain that much, even if it didn't bring her any sort of pleasure?

She searched the eyes of the man she had so quickly fallen for. Would he provide her some sort of an answer? He seemed dumbfounded, wordless. In his eyes, she found what she needed to. He was ashamed and there were tears hidden within those light emeralds.

He ran from her, but she followed. Her thigh was sore, a drop of blood fell on his slick hardwood floors. You could almost hear it until Jennifer belted out, "Anthony, wait!"

She found him in the kitchen, rummaging through a cabinet that hid first aid supplies. He had fished out some gauze and bandages and antibiotic ointment. Words weren't in the forecast for the moment. He had none. He kneeled before her, tears falling as he held onto both of her hands. He kissed each knuckle as well as her palms before spinning her around. Reaching to grab the gauze he had wetted down with water off the counter, he cleaned her wound that he'd inflicted. This made her flinch as it stung and burned with his gentle rubbing. He then reached for the antibiotic ointment and a large bandage, applying the goop before covering the small cut with a bandage. He placed a kiss over the bandage and flooded the backs of her legs with more kisses, trailing from her thighs to the fold of her buttcheek where her booty and thighs met. He then went lower, even turning her back over and kissing her feet. It was a shock to see such a leader of men bent before her and brought so low. It broke her.

She scrambled to her knees, humbled by his humiliation. She crawled into his arms, hungry for closeness with him. He had been far from her for too long. She was sobbing and his tears had finally come to a finale. He just held onto her tightly as if he would never be able to hold her again. Maybe, he thought he might not be able to. Did he think she would leave him?

Between pants of tears, Jennifer made her proclamation, "Anthony, I-I- love you. I don't care anymore. I know you're sorry. You didn't keep going after I used my safe word."

"How could you love me after that, Jenn? I snapped, I don't even remember giving you that- that cut. What if I hadn't stopped?"

"We don't need to question that. And it wasn't a gash, it's a nick and you stopped, which is all that matters. Maybe, we can take some anger management classes together? I could use them too. What even made you so angry to begin with?"

"It was the combination of you being irresponsible, my grandpa being so cruel, your friends and family taking advantage of you, the way you spoke to me in the car about needing to go to school... I'm sorry, Jenn."

His apology was punctuated with him lunging for her mouth, desperate for her taste. She gasped as she met his lips with her own, surprised by the passion with which he kissed her. They were two, connected completely to make one. Their kisses echoed the others and moved in a loving synchronicity. They were made for each other. Jenn's understanding and Anthony's command made for a delicious blend of personalities.

Anthony removed his pants and was quickly on top of Jenn, cock gliding right into her wet folds, even their bodies fit perfectly together like pieces of a puzzle. She was his little harlot and she couldn't be prouder. He made missionary sexy, smacking into her thick hips repeatedly. He had her screaming in pleasure within seconds. The sound of them crashing into each other like waves made music throughout the kitchen. He went from kissing her neck to sucking her nipples, even clamping down to gently bite once in a while, making her body shake.

His mouth felt so good against her hot, damp skin. She pressed the palms of her hands to the tile, holding herself in place as close to him as possible. He grabbed the hair at the crown of her head with both hands, one on each side, pulling harder with each stroke. He had her climaxing much faster than anyone had before. It felt like a haze came over her and she found herself shaking uncontrollably, sweat suctioning her to the flooring. This forced him to pull her hair even tighter to keep her from shaking away from him. He let out his own groan of pleasure as he allowed his cum to shoot deep inside her, his balls smacking into her pussy lips as they orgasmed together.

The two lovers lay together on the kitchen floor naked and wrapped up in the other. Jennifer played with Anthony's fingertips, tangling and untangling her hand from his. Anthony pressed a tiny, warm kiss to the side of Jenn's forehead before letting out a satisfied sigh. Both sat with sleepy smiles, neither eager for the moment to be over. However, there were pressing matters to discuss.

"What am I gonna do with you?" Anthony asked as he laughed at the predicament she was in.

"Yeah... by the way, there's more." Jennifer still hadn't told him about the photo evidence she was sent or about what had happened to Lola's hair the day before and why. She let it all out like word vomit and the two were laughing hysterically at her misfortune by the end of the telling. It was much easier to laugh about it than the other option: cry. Could her luck get any worse? What was she meant to learn from all of this? How was she supposed to grow?

"Well, little lady, if I'm about to help you with all of this and if I'm gonna be taking care of you, I think you're gonna need to start referring to me as 'Daddy'." His tone made it sound like he was teasing, but knowing Anthony, he was probably serious.

"Are you joking?" Jenn scoffed at the thought. Calling him 'Sir' had made her feel silly enough. How would calling him 'Daddy' make her feel?

"Nope, I'm serious. If you want my help out of this mess, call me Daddy." He had a smile spread across his face. He was serious, but obviously knew she would resist— at first.

"I do want your help... Daddy, but I have no clue how you could possibly help me out of this mess." Even as she said it, she cringed which had Anthony busting out in a belly laugh.

Once his laughter subsided, he responded, "You'll get used

to it eventually, my dear, and you'd be surprised just what I can do. For one, I'm giving you my credit card until your next pay day. From now on, any purchase that isn't food, rent, or gas needs to be run by me... especially while you're using my card."

"I can't just take your credit card and why should I have to run my decisions by you once it's back to my money? It's my money. You don't own me, Anthony." She felt herself getting fired up. Sure, she didn't make the best choices with her money, but he couldn't control her. She pulled away from him and sat up, ready for a fight. Anthony chose to stay calm and think about how cute she was when she was irritated with him.

"You'll still have your free will, but this way, I can help you decide if people are swindling you or not. Maybe, I'll advise you not to purchase a certain pair of shoes or something, but that would just be because I wanna buy that for you myself."

"I guess when you put it that way, that doesn't sound so bad. What about everything else?"

Anthony wasn't quite sure himself how he would fix everything or if he even could. All he knew was he was going to try to save his girl with all he had in him. Handling the petty stylists who were picking on Jenn would be easy. All he needed to do was text Monica to arrange a meeting and he would scare those women shitless. Maybe, he'd fire a couple of people to prove his point. He didn't care.

What wouldn't be so easy was trying to find the owner of that nasty photo of Jenn at the club. So many people had been there that night. Sure, he personally knew most of them, but how do you start that conversation? It was viewed as highly disrespectful to take a camera phone out in a place like that.

Photos were prohibited. Period. It had to have been someone pretty ballsy to go ahead and do it anyway. They could be completely banned from all of the kink clubs in the area. If only he knew who it was... his blood was boiling thinking of what he'd like to do to that person.

He was on his way to the club right now. He thought that talking to the dungeon masters and bouncers might prove useful. As he pulled in and parked, his mind went on autopilot and in just minutes, he found himself inside the packed BDSM club. Instead of discussing his intention with the bouncer at the front, he shoved his way through the entrance. Stomping his way to the mic with the bouncer on his tail. However, the bouncer recognized Anthony and only half-heartedly followed after him, possibly afraid to upset the powerful man.

Turning to address his pursuer, he barked out his command. "Turn. The. Music. Off." Anthony found it funny how afraid the man was. For such a big man, he was a pussy.

Grabbing the mic and flashing his phone screen, Anthony interrogated the entire room. "Who the fuck did this?" Anthony questioned, his fury rising.. He showed the entire room the photo of Jennifer. If they hadn't been there that night, it didn't matter. Someone had to know something.

One nasty looking man immediately started laughing. He had teeth that were rotting and a curly, black, unkempt beard. He was dressed in all leather. He looked like the sort of man who was carrying around numerous STDs. His teeth that weren't rotting were a dark shade of yellow. The whites of his eyes carried the same waxy shade.

"I may have seen that photo before, but fuck if I'm going to tell the likes of you, Daddy Big Bucks. Your money don't mean nothing to me, but I'll definitely take that little one off your hands since you can't seem to handle her yourself."

With that comment, Anthony was gone and in his place

was the Pitbull. He jumped across the room towards the man. First, pulling his beard to smack his head into the flooring. From there, Anthony got on top of him and began smashing his fist repeatedly into the man's disgusting face. He punched and punched at lightning speed. There was blood everywhere: on his shirt, his fists, his face. He could no longer see the oaf's features. All that could be seen was red and that's all he saw as he was pulled off of him and dragged out the back door to the alley where he was left to sort out his own rage.

Who had that man been and who did he know?

Chapter 10

There wasn't much else Jenn could do about the photo besides sit and wait. Anthony had hired an actual private investigator to try and figure out the name of the man he ran into at the club. Of course, he had left out the full details of the encounter when relating the tale to Jenn. After the accidental event during her last spanking, to try and tell her he might have sent a stranger to the emergency room didn't seem like the best idea. He was beginning to love her and didn't want her to run away or always be afraid of him.

They both wanted to push everything aside because it was time for the Giuliani Hair Convention, which happened once a year in Las Vegas. Every single Giuliani salon in the United States would be there and there would be classes on everything from nails to balayage to business. It was the event to be at. Anthony sure as hell couldn't miss it as he gave the opening toast every year. Jenn also felt she couldn't miss it. With all the stylists from the San Francisco area hating on her, this was a great opportunity for her to make friends, let people see the real her, and get to know her beyond the new girl who's apparently out to get Maybella.

Anthony had helped her pack her suitcase. They had gone to the mall and bought her new outfits for the event. She needed a few cocktail dresses for every night after all the learning was over as well as comfortable and professional outfits for during the day, something that showed her style and personality but wouldn't be difficult to sit in for long hours while learning. They had also bought her something that had been on her wish list for a crazy long time: the baby pink and rose gold Ted Baker bow suitcase. It would be so perfect for their first trip together.

The one thing that had her really nervous was wondering how they would hide their relationship. Sure, they had come out to Monica and Maybella already, but Anthony had told Maybella not to run her mouth or she'd pretty much be fired. Coming out to just two Giuliani employees was nothing in comparison with the number of staff that would be in attendance. They would have to sneak around in a way, which could be hot or it could be really stressful.

The best part would be getting to ride in Anthony's private jet, just the two of them. At one point, Momma and Papa Giuliani had discussed traveling with them. Anthony must have talked them out of it, which was a huge relief. She was pretty sure most of the family knew about their relationship, but since meeting Anthony's grandfather, she wasn't eager to spend time with any of them. She knew it would have to happen eventually, but she was savoring the time before that would be required. She was just thankful to be flying with him. Many of the other stylists were flying economy somewhere on the same plane together, but she had heard of groups that would be carpooling the ten-hour drive. Of course, nobody had invited her, but she was happy to say they hadn't. Would she rather spend ten hours in a car with bitches who hated her or an hour in a private jet with her man? It wasn't a tough decision.

Gerard was loading their suitcases onto the plane, hers pink and his black.

"Ant– er, Daddy… will Gerard be coming with us?" Jenn questioned with heat flooding her cheeks, hoping to God Gerard hadn't heard what she had called him.

"Yes, baby. We'll need someone to drive us around Vegas when you get done with your classes every night."

"But what will he drive with the Bentley left at the hangar?"

"Don't you worry about that, dear."

Stepping onto Anthony's jet was like stepping into a whole new world. It had Anthony written all over it. It was like a smaller version of his loft. Everything was black and white, leather and lush. He even had a fireplace and a chess table! If only she knew how to play chess… There was bench seating that encircled the chess table, which Anthony immediately took a seat on. He watched with hungry eyes as Jenn entered further into the space.

"So? What do you think?"

"I still can't believe you have a private jet."

"Would you like me to pinch you to see if you're dreaming? Or maybe spank you instead?"

Jenn came to sit near him, her arm stretched over the back of the bench. She was facing him with her knees and heels tucked beneath her. She looked into Anthony's eyes with the same hunger. Her own small shred of dominance coming out with the comfortability of being with him.

"Why do you enjoy spanking me so much?"

"I like spanking you because I can feel how wet you are for me when I fuck you after."

Just then, a man dressed like a caterer came out from the back of the plane. Jenn had a feeling this man had just heard everything that was said. He held a bottle of Dom Perignon and two champagne flutes in the other hand.

"Champagne, Monsieur? Mademoiselle?"

"*Merci beaucoup*, Guillaume."

The man proceeded to pour each of them a glass before walking backwards to his original hiding place. Leaving the couple to drink bubbles and finish their previous discussion on the matters of motivation towards masochists.

"I apologize, my dear, Guillaume only speaks French."

"And apparently you do too! I had no idea." At least she knew Guillaume had not heard, or rather, understood their intimate conversation.

"I'm fluent in both French and Italian. You know, many big hair names were launched from France. It'd be good for you to learn too."

Leaning in to place a sweet champagne kiss to his lips, Jenn replied, "Well, maybe you should teach me."

As he kissed her, he placed his hand at the front of her neck. He massaged her throat and esophagus, teasing her with the thought of being choked. This had always scared her before, but she trusted Anthony because she knew he knew what he was doing. Maybe, when they were fully alone, she might allow him to choke her for real. For now, she reminisced about the kiss, enjoying the harshness of it. He even bit her lip, producing a soft moan. How badly she wished Guillaume wasn't there.

"You like that, don't you, little minx?" Anthony gently teased his lady about her obvious arousal. She just smiled and leaned in further to kiss him a little bit longer.

Anthony pulled back and gestured to the rest of the jet's interior. "Is this everything you imagined a private jet experience to be? Is there anything else you'd like to do before we land? I do believe we are running out of time."

"Hmm, can we have any snacks? Is Guillaume hiding a snack somewhere in his little corner?"

At the sound of his name rolling off of her American lips,

Guillaume returned. He was eager and ready to serve in whatever way possible.

"Mademoiselle?"

"Guillaume, *les fraises s'il vous plait*." Her daddy made the response that she was unable to.

Looking at her and raising his eyebrows for emphasis, he explained, "A snack for my snack."

Guillaume immediately returned with a crystal platter of the most beautifully decorated chocolate covered strawberries Jenn had ever seen in all her life and she had consumed plenty. There was white and milk and dark chocolate galore. There were even a few that were pink from white chocolate and red food coloring. Some were drizzled in stripes and a few had sprinkles that looked like little, edible pearls. Her favorites were in the center of the platter, with just one decoration: dark chocolate dipped and drizzled with pink and white chocolate into the shape of a rose. The French attendant placed the tray on the seat before clearing the pieces from the chess table before them, putting them into a small felt bag and placing them on the shelf beneath. He left behind their two, empty champagne glasses. Then, Guillaume moved the tray to the center of their focus, the chess table. He went to the back and quickly returned with the Dom Perignon, refilling their flutes.

They finished off the last of the strawberries just as they felt the plane swoop and begin descending. They'd be in Vegas in just a few minutes! Jenn's tummy was so full of strawberries that the descent and turbulence sent her full of butterflies.

"Daddy, I'm scared."

Anthony scooted closer to her on the slick leather seating, completely folding her into his strong and capable arms. He squeezed her as tight as he could. His fragrance flooded her senses and calmed her in a way that no other aromatherapy ever could.

"You're safe with me, darling. You're always safe with me."

Jennifer and Anthony walked up the marble front steps of the hotel that he had booked for them weeks ago. The white and gray swirls beneath them glimmered in the bright Las Vegas afternoon sun. They walked in sync, one step after the other. Jenn's pink pumps clicked with each elevated footstep. She felt like she was losing herself in a daydream rather than reality, but her heart murmured with the fear somebody might see the two of them entering the hotel together to check into one room. She knew most of the stylists from her salon had chosen a cheaper spot down the road as opposed to the glamorous hotel where the convention was being hosted, but it didn't matter. She was still afraid to be seen. However, she noticed Anthony didn't seem to care at all. She found this strange because wasn't he the one with the bigger reputation to protect? Why wasn't he more worried what his employees would think? Jenn would give anything to have his 'I don't give a fuck' stance. She gave altogether too many.

Two bellhops held the gold-trimmed front doors wide open for the couple. They entered through to an entirely new universe. The ceilings were high and painted in an exact replica of the Sistine Chapel. Jenn stood with her neck craned towards the sky for a second longer than most would. She was lost in it. It was so beautiful and her breath and her voice had deserted her.

Anthony tugged on her arm towards the expansive front desk and cleared his throat. "What do you think? Let's get ourselves checked in, yeah?"

She tried as hard as she could to seem grown up and collected as the front desk receptionist went over all the identity confirmation questions with Anthony, but she couldn't help herself. She was enthralled, captivated by her surroundings. There was a grand piano and table after table set up for the conference. It actually looked more like a ballroom than a hotel lobby and it made Jenn wonder how the real ballroom could possibly top this room in beauty.

The small girl behind the desk had just given Anthony the keys to the presidential suite when the front doors were once again opened wide. This time showing off a much bitchier entourage. There standing before them was Maybella and her little posse of stylists, some of whom still worked at the same location as Jenn. She sharply inhaled as she felt the pit in her stomach, which had been there since they landed, drop to the floor. Here was her biggest fear coming true in just a matter of seconds after they had entered the hotel. She at least thought they'd be able to keep themselves hidden a day or two.

Anthony broke her out of her thoughts by pridefully taking her small hand in his and leading her towards the elevator. They stepped onto the lift in silence. It was one of those elevators made of glass so they were able to watch the group of girls staring them down until they were to the next floor and out of view. It was the longest elevator ride she had ever been on in her life as their room was to be found on the very top floor, the 53rd to be exact. Neither said a word. Anthony was in a calm silence, while Jenn let her mind reel and spin out of control.

As they watched the red, technological number flip from 49 to 50, Jenn felt a tear fall off her cheek. Anthony noticed immediately, grabbed her by her shoulders and made her face him. She looked into his crystal-like eyes. She looked away just to have Anthony hook a finger under her chin, forcing her to hold eye contact with him.

"Hey... do not let them ruin this trip for you or for us. They have nothing on you."

This made Jenn lose it. Tears ran down her face as she yelled at him.

"*Unless one of them is behind that damn photo. They could have a lot on me!* Why don't you get it, Anthony?" Jenn yelled at him, knowing her irritation was misdirected.

The red number switched to 53 and the elevator doors glided open. Anthony grabbed Jenn possessively by the wrist and pulled tighter as he used his grip to encourage her closer to their suite. He only let go to slide the key through the door lock, but immediately grabbed her wrist back and yanked her into the room.

He slammed the door and began to calmly, but firmly, put Jennifer back in her place.

"For one, you are to refer to me as Daddy as we've previously discussed. You don't call me Anthony. Sir would've been okay, but you've chosen to push the wrong buttons on me. Also, for your information, the private investigator found that man's name, San Antonio Black. We are just waiting to discover his tie to us, but we're sure he's the one who took the photo."

Jennifer took three deep breaths, in through her nose and out through her mouth. She was trying to find some sort of serenity though she fully knew what was coming... what she needed and what she deserved.

Anthony was already sitting at the foot of their California king bed with his arms out. She knew what to do and immediately began to make her way towards him. She didn't want to provoke him any further and was already sorry for doing so in the first place. She thought it was crazy, even when she was fearful of him, his energy pulled her closer. She couldn't resist him if she wanted to.

As Jenn bent to lie across Anthony's lap he grunted in disapproval. Jenn was taken aback, literally. She stepped away from him with confusion in her eyes. If he didn't want to spank her, what did he intend to do?

"On your knees, little slut."

Fear and trembling overcame her. She kneeled before him, apprehensive. He had never had her do anything like this before and the unknown overwhelmed her. More tears came out since the elevator. Would they ever stop or simply stop and start forever?

She got onto her knees and did the one thing any good submissive knows how to do. She folded her hands on her lap and bent her head low, focal point angled at the lush carpeting. She listened as Anthony rose to his feet, now towering far over her.

"Look at me." She flinched at the sting behind his tone, but did as she was told. She made eye contact with him and only held his gaze for a moment before feeling a stinging pain come over her face. She clamped her eyes shut for a split second. She gasped both from pain and surprise at being slapped across the face. She knew all she needed to do for it all to stop was use her safe word, but she wasn't one-hundred-percent sure if she wanted it to ever stop. One thing she knew for certain. She wasn't going to look up at him, unless he commanded her to.

Her senses were heightened from fright and anticipation. It felt as if the sound of Anthony quickly unsnapping his belt and allowing the metal and his pants buttons to click to the floor was amplified. She winced at the noise, half terrified he would spank her with the belt he had removed. He snatched the hair at her hairline and pushed back. This forced her to look up at his hard cock which he had untucked from his Versace boxers which had a banding lined with gold and Swarovski crystals and with, of course, the iconic lion emblem.

With his other hand he grabbed her by the jaw, forcing her to pooch her lips in a fishlike way. "Open your mouth."

She obeyed as Daddy wanted.

He immediately shoved his dick into her mouth, jamming himself deep within her throat. This made her gag, hard, but he didn't retract. Rather, he used the hand that was in her hair to further bob her head back and forth on his stiff arousal. She was completely without control. Her face belonged to him and all she could do was relax her esophagus as much as possible and open her mouth wide. Her eyes watered, but he had just begun to reach his climax. He removed himself from her as he spread his cum over her eager mouth and outstretched tongue. She had cum all over her face, but she didn't care. It was the most fun she had had with her man up until this point.

As soon as he came, he tucked his cock back into his boxers. Then, he went to the suite's large luxurious bathroom to grab one of the fluffy white towels.

He gently wiped all of his milky secretion from her face in an upward and outward motion, while questioning her.

"You enjoyed that a lot, didn't you, princess?"

Shit, so it had been obvious.

By the time they had finished cleaning each other up and showering, it was time to get ready for the opening cocktail party and for the arrival toast Anthony would be giving. Anthony was wearing a navy flannel suit with a white button up and black shoes. Jenn was in a short, black sequined dress, a poofy faux fur jacket, and silver open-toed heels.

Together they entered the lobby where the first event was being held, but Jenn separated from Anthony as soon as possible. She was still horrified at the thought of what people may or may not think of her after they found out the truth. She didn't want to think of the assumptions people would make.

The room was buzzing with the amount of people present and Jenn found herself feeling uncomfortable and out of place. Everyone else was a part of some sort of clique they had traveled with. She watched Anthony from across the room, tangled in one conversation after the next. Everyone wanted a chance to talk to Mr. Giuliani while his woman sat by herself, with a Cosmopolitan, in the corner. She felt like running back to her hotel room, but knew she needed to try to put herself out there and talk to somebody.

Resolutely, she walked up to one of the tall tables that had chattering hairstylists standing circled around it. As she walked up, the conversation stopped for a split second before continuing on, leaving Jenn without an opportunity to introduce herself. They were discussing all the classes they were planning to attend the next few days. When Jenn made an attempt to share how excited she was for the texture workshop, she was spoken over. It wasn't in a rude way; everyone was just super pumped. It didn't help to make Jennifer feel any more comfortable, though. She downed her cosmopolitan and went to grab another.

The lobby was long and narrow with the entrance to the hotel at one of the far ends and a large, plain wall with a projector facing it at the other. The bar stretched across the right wall.

Jenn anxiously kicked her feet and fidgeted with the bottom of her skirt as she waited in line at the bar, listening in on the conversations happening around her. Everyone was networking and excited to be there. Everyone except for her. She had never felt more out of place and she desperately wished Lola, McKayla, and Steph could've been there with her. Would she ever make a friend at Giuliani's?

Suddenly, she was embraced from behind, arms wrapping

around her fur covered shoulders. She couldn't see who it was at first so she was startled and her anxiety made her feel like she was being attacked rather than hugged. She turned around with her hands already forming into fists, ready to defend herself. Surprised at who she found, she returned the eager greeting as she threw her arms around Monica. She was so unbelievably grateful to see a kind, familiar face. It seemed as if she had been getting upset and lost in her feelings for nothing.

Monica leaned in and in a hushed, comrade-like way asked, "So... how was the private jet?"

This question and the way in which it was asked made Jenn break it into a big smile, wanting to laugh at how Monica was acting as if she were a spy asking their partner about some top secret information. She quickly filled Monica in on every-thing from the chess table to Guillame to the strawberries. Time flew by and they soon found the long line they had origi-nally been standing in had grown quite short and they were ordering their drinks within minutes.

Monica led Jenn back to the table she was sitting at which just so happened to have Momma and Papa Giuliani seated at it as well as Anthony along with a few other people she didn't know. The Giuliani's all greeted her with a knowing smile, careful not to blow their cover, however. It was kind of fun pretending there was nothing going on between them when really they were obsessed with one another.

Monica introduced her to the few people she hadn't known. It wasn't long before Anthony began checking his watch. He would be going up to give his toast at 7:30. The third time he checked was the right time. Jenn watched as he untucked himself from the table and made his way towards the other side of the room, where the projector and micro-phone were. As he walked, he was watched by his lover as she admired every bit of him. Even the way he walked commanded attention because he did so with pride and with confidence. Monica gently kicked her under the table before giving her the eyes that only a friend could read, eyes that said 'Cut it out. You're being obvious'.

Anthony switched the projector to his first slide, which simply said, "Welcome." He cleared his throat and looked out over the room of employees. He caught eyes with Jenn who gave him an encouraging nod and smile, even though he didn't really need it. It felt so good to not have to be a lone wolf anymore, to have somebody in his corner. He returned her smile before speaking.

"Good evening, everyone! I'm Anthony Giuliani, one of the owners of the Giuliani franchise. If you haven't ever met me before, please search me out and pull me to the side. I hope to have met every single one of you by the end of this weekend. Now, I would like to propose a toast- to hair and to expanding our knowledge of it!"

He raised his glass to the enormous room, encouraging the audience to do the same. It seemed like every single person participated. They all raised their glasses and shouted out, "To hair!" as if there was a competition going on of who could shout the loudest.

He then began to flip through his other slides that went over all the times of the classes, the after parties, as well as some of the themes for the after-hours events that would be going on. As he flipped to his next slide, something or someone took over. His slides wouldn't click through. The screen went black and Anthony couldn't help but look dumbfounded. He searched the room with his eyes for anyone who might know what was going on. They landed on one person: Maybella, who had a snarky look on her face.

The next thing that happened couldn't have been predicted by anyone and not very many people would be able to explain how it happened, but the screen now depicted something that Anthony had not planned. It was *the* photo, the one of Jenn getting her spanking from the dungeon master, splatted across the huge, far wall for anyone and everyone to see. Anthony stood with his mouth hanging open, not knowing what to do. The rest of the room wasn't sure how they were supposed to react. Most of them didn't recognize the girl in the picture and they didn't understand what it could have to do with hair.

At Jenn's table, however, there was a response. The few people she had just met stared at her, gawking as if waiting for her, or someone, or anyone to explain. Papa Giuliani cleared his throat while Momma Giuliani gently tapped Jenn on the shoulder much like how the Queen of England might pat a sick child. Monica immediately grabbed Jenn's hand under the table. For the first few moments, Jenn sat there, stunned. The entire room slowly began to turn to her as the realization of who was in the picture spread like wildfire. One table after the next turned to her for an answer. A table would all turn their heads, signaling to the table beside them that they should look in the same direction.

When Jenn finally snapped out of it and jumped up from the table, a loud robotic voice began to speak. She didn't hear a word it said as she ran and ran. She didn't know where she was going, but she couldn't wait for an elevator so she searched for the stairwell. When she found it, she began to climb.

Anthony had watched as Jenn got up and ran. He wanted to follow her, but he also knew he needed to hear what this ominous voice was about to say. He needed all the details to be able to clean up the mess that soon followed.

These were the words that projected and echoed throughout the entire room, "Anthony Giuliani is in an intimate relationship with this young employee, Jennifer Caman. They engage in these sorts of activities together. That is all."

"Go." This one command from his parents was all Anthony had needed. He would deal with the repercussions later. For now, he needed to save his baby. What kind of Daddy would he be if he couldn't comfort her through this?

Jennifer hadn't planned to hide in their suite because she wanted to be alone. She didn't want to look at Anthony because anything he had to say wouldn't make her feel any better. She didn't want to disappoint him. He wouldn't understand. She had just been forced to not only come out about her relationship with him, but also about her newfound love of kink. Anthony was already comfortable with himself and his sexual desires. She wasn't.

When she had made it to their suite, she searched for a hiding spot. She knew it wouldn't be long before he came looking for her and their suite would be the first place he would check. The best she could come up with was the closet. She quickly flung the door open and made her way to the back, the darkest part. She sat crouched beneath her pretty dresses, sobbing. What would the future of her career look like? Would everyone at Giuliani's always see her as the girl in the stocks, getting spanked? Could she even build a professional hair career now or would she need to go back to school? Would the bullying get so bad she would have to quit her job at Giuliani's? Maybe, she should just break up with Anthony. That would solve some of her problems.

Jenn listened as Anthony swung the hotel room door open.

"Jenn? Where are you? If you don't come out and talk to me, I will be giving you a spanking."

Should she risk it? The sound of her sobs just about blew her cover so she began taking slow and controlled deep breaths to calm herself down. She didn't want to look at him.

It wasn't his fault, but she did feel like Maybella was behind this. If it wasn't for Maybella and Anthony's history, none of this might be happening. She knew he would find her eventually. She listened as he threw things around, probably looking under the bed and in the bathroom first.

He opened the closet door, his voice broke as he asked for her.

"Jenn, baby, are you in there?" He moved the clothes, sliding over the long dresses that were keeping her hidden.

"What are you doing?" he asked as Jenn slowly climbed out, a bit embarrassed at herself for hiding from him.

"Why are you hiding from me?"

"You won't get it. I just want to be alone."

"Come to Daddy. It'll be okay."

Though she wanted to resist him, she couldn't with him sitting before her looking so broken. She crawled into his arms where he sat on the edge of the bed. He held her for a long time while she cried into his shoulder. He held her as tightly as he could, hoping he could squeeze her back together. A tear fell from his own eyes listening to her. She was so low and he didn't know how to build her back up. He waited until her breathing slowed and her tears came to an end. There was no telling how long they sat there. He couldn't rush her and he knew that. He knew what had happened would impact her more than it did him. She cared so deeply what people thought of her. He had never been that way.

"Talk to me, baby. What's going through your head?" Anthony softly questioned, hoping for some response, some way to feel connected to her again.

"What am I going to do, Daddy?"

"You don't need to do anything. You haven't done anything wrong. You don't need to explain yourself. Let's just own it. This is a good thing. Everyone knows about us now so we don't have to hide it for the rest of the trip. I can introduce you to all the people I know."

Anthony's words affected her in a way she hadn't expected. Something inside of her finally clicked. She wasn't doing anything wrong. Why should she feel the need to apologize for who she loved or how she loved? She knew she had to own it. Most of her worries had been constructed by herself. If she hadn't cared what Katie thought, would she have run away that night? She would've just let everything Katie had said roll off her shoulders. She wouldn't have spent so much money on other people, so desperate for those around her to like her. Her job up until this point would have had a lot less stress because she wouldn't have been so afraid of what Maybella could say or do. Why should she be hiding in a closet on the most amazing trip of her life? She had done nothing wrong.

At that moment, there was a knock on the door and Anthony left her to get up and see who it was. He opened the door wide to let his parents in. His mom came to Jenn's side and wrapped her arms around the young girl.

"I am so sorry our staff have been bullying you. Do not let anything they say affect how you feel about yourself. We love you. I handpicked you myself and I couldn't be more proud to have you dating our son. He has changed since being with you. He's brighter now."

Momma Giuliani loved on Jenn, brushing her hair from her face and grabbing her a tissue. Papa Giuliani, a man of few words, stood beside Anthony and slowly nodded his head. He had a gleam of warmth within his eyes. He agreed with his wife.

Anthony looked down at his phone when a text had pinged across the screen.

"It's the investigator. He says San Antonio Black is Maybella's brother-in-law."

Momma Giuliani looked from Anthony back to Jenn and said the last thing she had to say on the matter, "We addressed the masses, but Papa Giuliani and I think you and Anthony should do so as well, even if you just stand by Anthony while he does the talking."

"I think I have something I'd like to say," Jenn replied.

Anthony and Jenn stood where Anthony had stood about an hour ago. The room had gotten rowdier since having a few more drinks and it was hard to quiet them down. Jenn couldn't help but notice that it seemed most people had forgotten about them already.

Anthony started them off.

"I would like to start by apologizing. That was highly unprofessional and now that I know the person who made that happen, there will be serious repercussions. We can keep this short and simple. Yes, Jennifer and I are together and I'm proud to be seen with her. I won't allow either of us to be questioned about our relationship. Furthermore, what we do in our free time outside of the workplace has nothing to do with any of you, and I'm sorry to all of you and to Jenn that you saw that photo of her. That was unfair to her."

Jenn saw it was her turn and she took it.

"And I would like to say I refuse to be ashamed for who I love or how we choose to love one another. Thank you."

She was shocked by the audience's response, they erupted in cheering and claps.

Anthony entered the dimly lit presidential suite with what Jenn had come to think of as his 'game face'. She used the term 'game' because that look of mischief always seemed to mean sexy playtime was about to begin. Not saying anything, he leaned over and scooped her into his strong arms, bridal style. Taking her over to the large rug at the center of the room, he bent over again, but this time to set her down onto the floor. He knelt in front of her in order to make eye contact. This got the heat rising to her ears. Every ounce of that intensity was being focused on her as he said the words that proved she had been correct.

"You're about to be really naughty for me, baby. I've planned something for us to celebrate. I was so proud of you tonight." His green eyes glittered in jest as if to say he had something special for her up his sleeve. She loved that about him. He was always coming up with something new for her to try. She knew beyond a shadow of a doubt they could be together forty plus years, but their sex would never get boring.

"You still trust me one-hundred-percent, correct?" Those gorgeous greens went from mischievous to searching within seconds. She was aware she must respond quickly. He didn't like having to wait for anything so she nodded.

"I want you to use your words." With the command, his eyes turned from searching to frustrated. She should have learned by now.

"Yes, Daddy. I trust you one-hundred-percent." Her heart had already begun racing and excitement rippled throughout her entire being.

"And you remember your safe word?" How could she forget? It was impossible to think of a more ridiculous safe word than 'apricots'.

"Yes, Daddy." She attempted to hide her giggle.

"And you *will* use the safe word if it needs to be used?" The one issue that had been coming up for them was Jennifer refusing to say her safe word, even though she knew she should. She wanted to push herself and seem strong or experienced when that was not the case at all.

"Yes, Daddy." She didn't want to disappoint Anthony again. Face falling, she picked at her fingernails that were painted a bright purple, his favorite color.

"Get undressed."

They both stood and her hands shook as she pulled her dress up and over her head, tossing it aside. She hesitated at the waistband of her panties. "Everything?" she asked, her confidence leaving her, this question was laced with anxiety. He was watching her undress with his bulging arms crossed and his expression inscrutable.

"Everything, baby." A hint of a smile escaped by accident as he was trying to do his usual stern approach. She made him behave in a way he never had with any sub in the past. He watched as she slid her seamless thong down her thighs and to her ankles, stepping out of them. The next thing to go was her bralette. She didn't like padding so all it had to it was a bit of lavender colored lace and underwire. She reached behind her back and managed to undo the clasp with one quivering hand. Kicking her panties to the edge of the room, she added the bralette to the pile.

As soon as she was made bare before him, Anthony barked out, "On your knees." Jenn knew exactly how he meant and did as she was told, relaxing her hands on her thighs, palms up and head bent to face the ground.

"Good girl." She couldn't help but think how cute it was that he was trying hard to not seem excited. He was like a giddy parent on Christmas morning, buzzing to see the look on his children's faces when they opened their gifts. Of course, she would never allow him to know what she was thinking. All jokes aside there's something to be said about being naked in front of your partner like this while he was still fully dressed. It made her feel liberated, strong and excited and most of all, desirable.

Anthony turned and reached to open the bedroom door and, as he did so, in stepped a man who was on the same level as the hulk. Where had he found him? The man was in nothing besides a pair of tight briefs and it looked as if he had stuffed them, but she had a sneaking suspicion that there were no illusions here. It was all real. He was by all human standards a sight of perfection, chiseled by the gods to make women's pussies drip. Washboard abs aside, the best thing about him was his long, black, curly hair. She knew now wasn't the time to be thinking about things like this, but her strongest urge in this moment was to style his hair, but Anthony had other orders set out for her.

Taking the armchair from the far corner of the room, Anthony dragged it across the glossy floor with ease so as to place it right in front of Jenn. He then went to stand by the Adonis.

"Jenn, Gregory here is going to remove his briefs and sit in the chair I've placed in front of you. His legs will be on either side of you. This is all because I've grown quite tired of how prideful you've become in regard to your infamous 'blowies' as you have taken to calling them. So, you're going to give Gregory a 'blowie' and while you're doing that, I'm going to spank you with my riding crop. How does that sound? Do you object to anything I've just described?"

She tried not to seem too excited, but he had just brought her the fantasy she wanted to try the most on a silver platter and she hadn't even had to tell him. He just knew.

Continuing to look at her hands, she made her response. "No, sir."

"Good girl. Do you remember which one is my riding crop?"

She nodded her head.

"Words, Jenn."

Oops. "Yes, Daddy."

"Yes, Daddy what?"

"Yes, Daddy. I do remember which one is your riding crop and I do not object to being spanked with it by you." She prayed to God he didn't catch the sass in her answer. She wasn't sure if she could handle this and another punishment afterwards.

"Good girl. Gregory, you may take your seat." The man removed his briefs and then did as he was told. Jenn had to admit it was really hot to see Anthony taking charge over the entire scene, Gregory included and not just Jenn this time.

It wasn't until this giant of a man sat in front of her with his massive, rock-solid dick in her face that she finally realized the overwhelming reality of the situation and then began overthinking. Giving a blowie would be nothing, but this man was way too big for her little mouth and she was going to be spanked at the same time? Sometimes, she couldn't take her spanking when nothing else was going on and she had nothing to physically do herself. How would she be able to work her magic? There was also the humiliating fact she was entirely naked in front of somebody she had never met. She wouldn't allow herself to feel dirty for wanting this anymore.

"Go on, baby girl. Do not leave Master Greg waiting." She hadn't realized it but during her inner monologue, Anthony had already gone to the wardrobe, retrieved the riding crop and positioned himself, standing on his knees behind her. Ready to go. With this comment, he made the first swat, bouncing right off her ass quickly. That sound was always what got her pussy wet initially. The swat had been soft and could've been seen as more of an encouragement than a punishment. She loved that about him. He always knew when she needed reassurance, never judging her for needing it.

With the vote of confidence, she went for it, gently grabbing Greg's dick and popping it into her mouth first thing.

Anthony landed a hard smack across her right cheek and even though she knew it was coming, she let out a startled scream, but the scream was muffled by Greg's dick in her mouth. "Where's my 'yes Daddy'?" Anthony asked. The question was dotted with another rough smack and, after her squeal, she attempted to garble out, "Yes, Daddy". It must have been good enough because Anthony said nothing and continued spanking. Now, alternating between each cheek and between the intensity of the spanks. She managed to stop squealing every time, but tears were tickling their way down her cheeks and it took all the focus she could muster not to bite down onto Greg's dick in pain.

However, Jenn wasn't a selfish girl. She wouldn't give Master Greg the bare minimum in an attempt to spare herself. She gently held onto his balls and massaged as her saliva slid down his shaft to lubricate the manipulation. Jenn slid as far down as she could in an attempt to take as much of his cock into her throat. As she did this, she slid her tongue back and forth along the underside of the shaft. Just as her lips reached the base of his shaft and she started to head back to the tip, Anthony delivered a comparably harder smack than she had been used to. This sent her bobbing further onto Greg's dick than she meant, choking herself to the point where she was afraid she might gag. There wouldn't be a break for Jenn, however, Greg had his hands in her hair and used this time to thrust with his own hips further into her face. He did this repeatedly for a few minutes until there was so much saliva and tears that she was sure her makeup had to look insane. *At least men are usually into that*, she thought.

Once Greg decided to relax and let her finish doing her thing, she used the opportunity to use her hand to massage his dick in a petrissage motion while focusing on the tip with her mouth. She sucked until she felt it was getting boring and began to swirl circles along the rim between the tip and the shaft with the point of her tongue. She also took the time to flick over his dick hole a few times, all the while never forgetting Anthony's punishing presence.

When Greg came, she wasn't surprised when Anthony quickly ushered him out of the suite. When Anthony returned to the bedroom, she was waiting silently. He reached for her hands, pulled her to her feet, and showed her who she would always belong to.

She never thought she would find such happiness in her life. She would be thankful every day for Anthony's love and care. Her life with Anthony would hold endless possibilities and she was ready to accept and enjoy each one.

Blushing Books

Blushing Books is the oldest eBook publisher on the web. We've been running websites that publish steamy romance and erotica since 1999, and we have been selling eBooks since 2003. We have free and promotional offerings that change weekly, so please do visit us at http://www.blushingbooks.-com/free.

Blushing Books Newsletter

Please join the Blushing Books newsletter
to receive updates & special promotional offers.
You can also join by using your mobile phone:
Just text BLUSHING to 22828.

Every month, one new sign up via text messaging will receive
a $25.00 Amazon gift card, so sign up today!